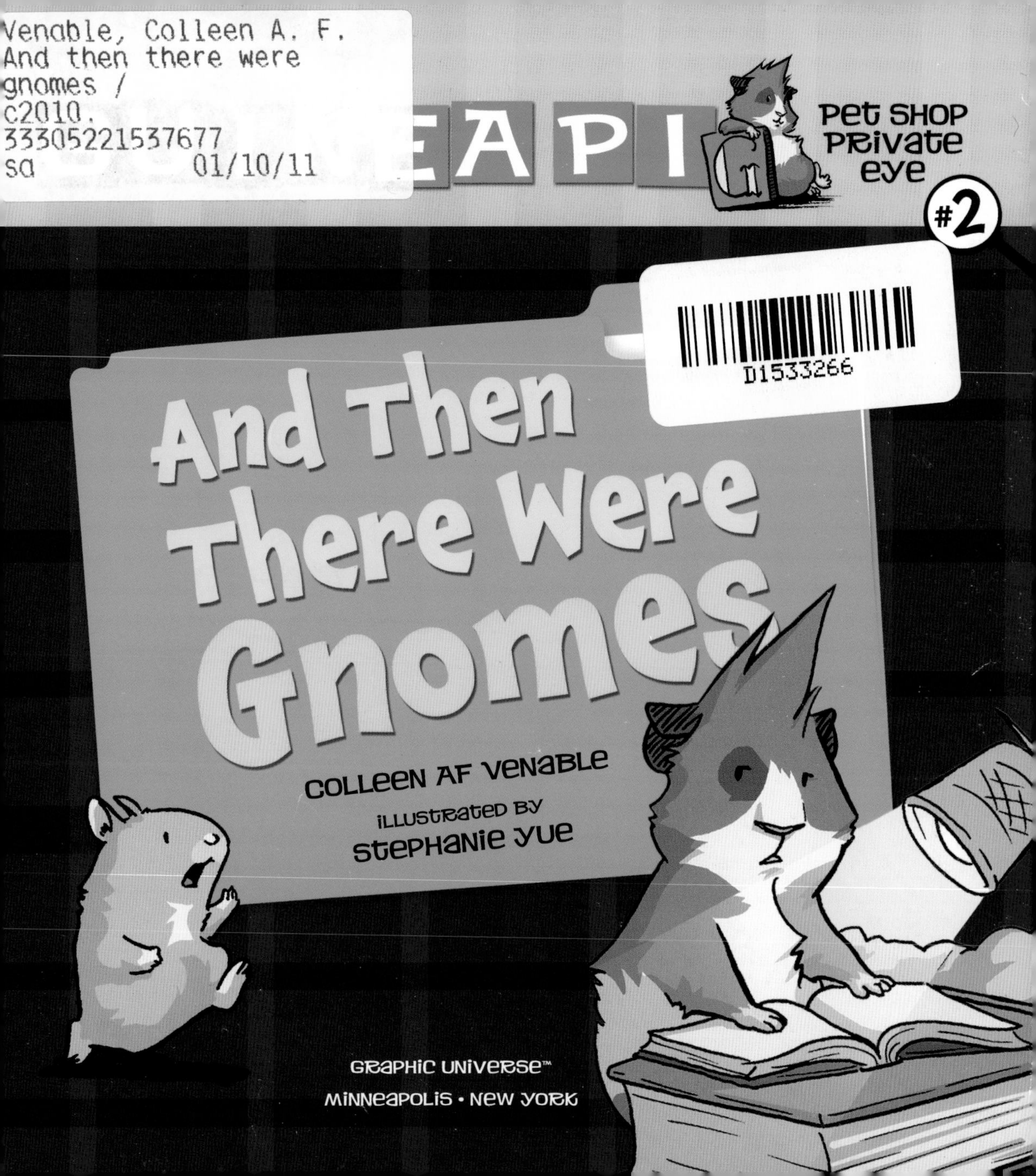
EAPI
G
Pet SHOP
PRivate
eye
#2
And Then
There Were
Gnomes
COLLEEN AF VENABLE
iLLUSTRATED BY
STEPHANIE YUE
GRAPHIC UNIVERSE™
MINNEAPOLIS • NEW YORK

Story by Colleen AF Venable

Art by Stephanie Yue

Coloring by Hi-Fi Design

Lettering by Zack Giallongo

Copyright © 2010 by Lerner Publishing Group, Inc.

Graphic Universe™ is a trademark of Lerner Publishing Group, Inc.

All rights reserved. International copyright secured. No part of this book may be reproduced, stored in a retrieval system, or transmitted in any form or by any means—electronic, mechanical, photocopying, recording, or otherwise—without the prior written permission of Lerner Publishing Group, Inc., except for the inclusion of brief quotations in an acknowledged review.

Graphic Universe™
A division of Lerner Publishing Group, Inc.
241 First Avenue North
Minneapolis, MN 55401 U.S.A.

Website address: www.lernerbooks.com

Library of Congress Cataloging-in-Publication Data

Venable, Colleen AF.
    And then there were gnomes / by Colleen AF Venable ; illustrated by Stephanie Yue.
      p. cm. — (Guinea PIG, pet shop private eye ; #02)
    Summary: Sasspants, the reluctant guinea pig private investigator, is drawn into another mystery by Hamisher the hamster who believes there is a ghost in the pet shop.
      ISBN: 978–0–7613–4599–2 (lib. bdg. : alk. paper)
      1. Graphic novels. [1. Graphic novels. 2. Mystery and detective stories. 3. Guinea pigs—Fiction. 4. Hamsters—Fiction. 5. Pet shops—Fiction. 6. Animals—Fiction. 7. Humorous stories.] I. Yue, Stephanie, ill. II. Title.
    PZ7.7.V46And 2010
    741.5'973—dc22   2009020896

Manufactured in the United States of America
1 – DP – 7/15/10

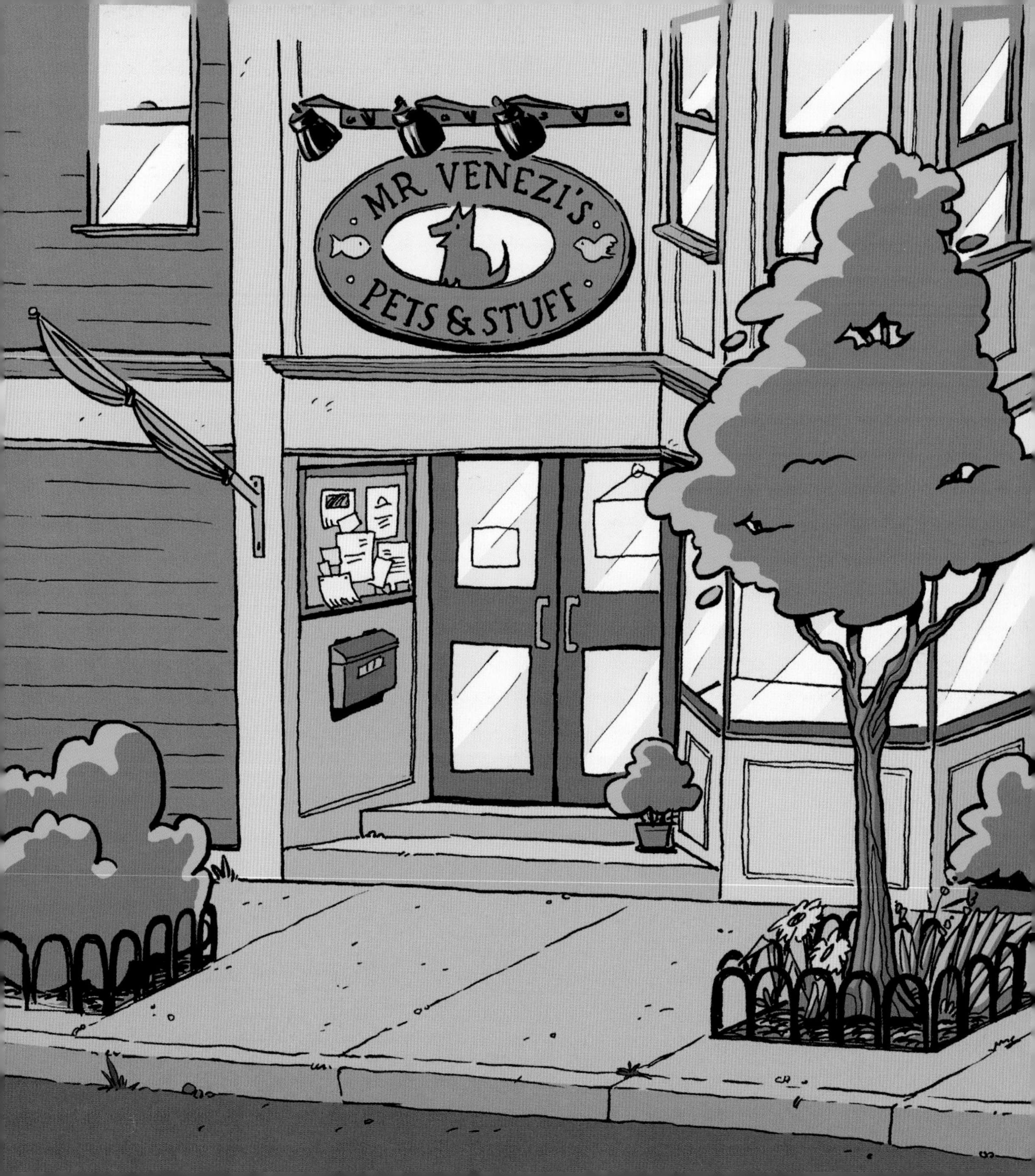
MR. VENEZI'S
PETS & STUFF

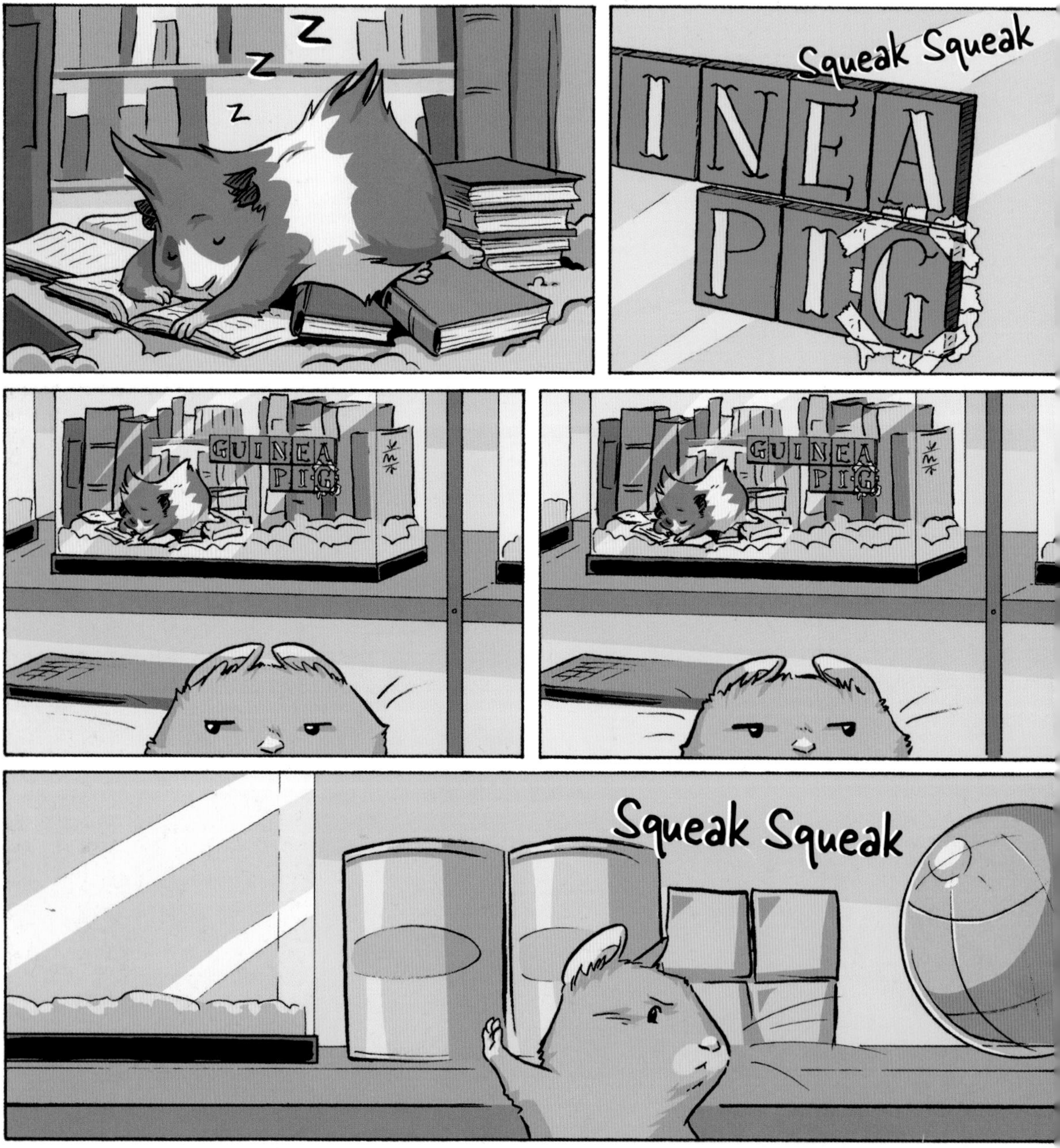
Z Z Z
Squeak Squeak
INEA
PIG
GUINEA
PIG
GUINEA
PIG
Squeak Squeak

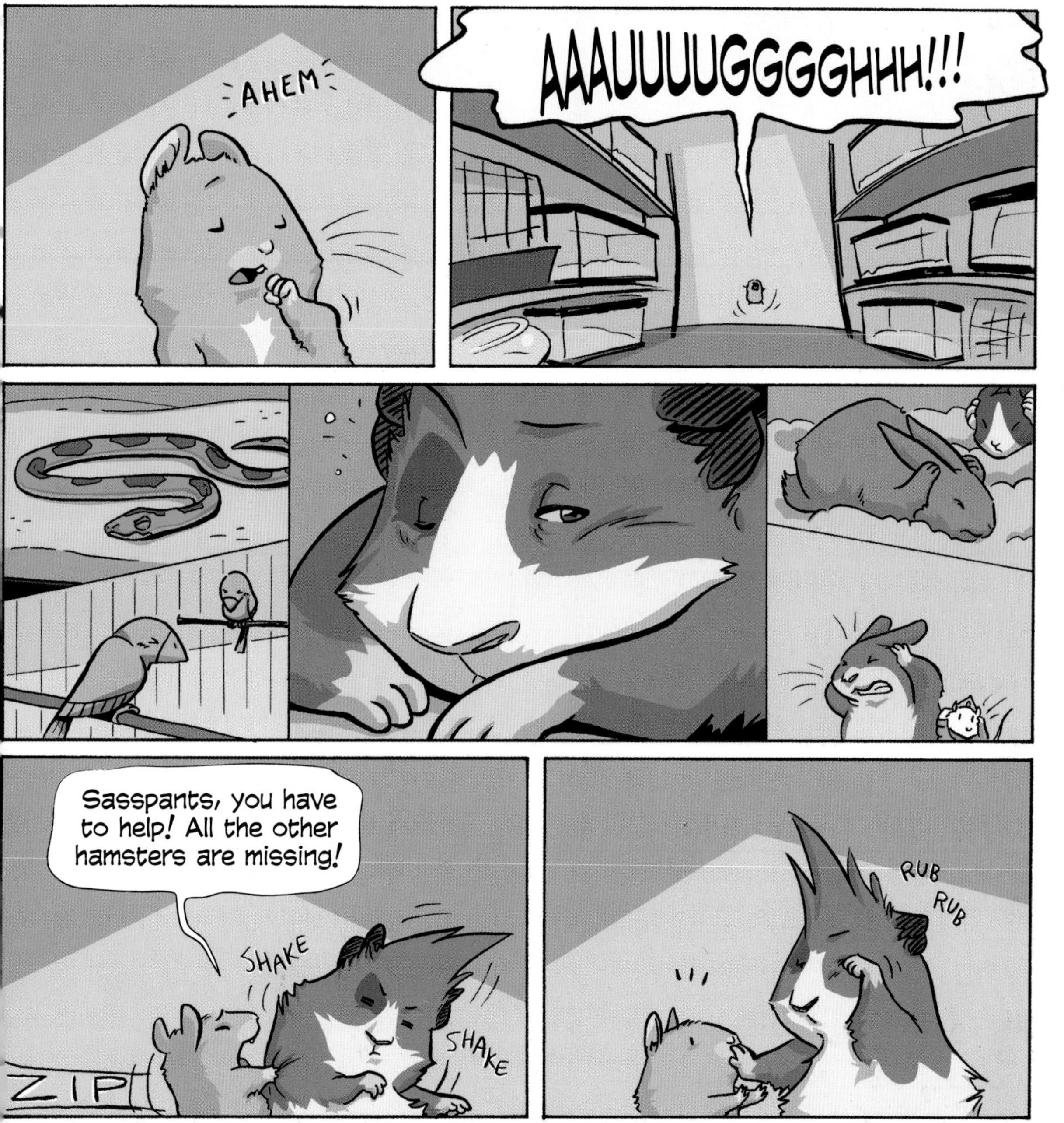
AHEM
AAAUUUUGGGGHHH!!!
Sasspants, you have to help! All the other hamsters are missing!
SHAKE
SHAKE
ZIP
RUB RUB

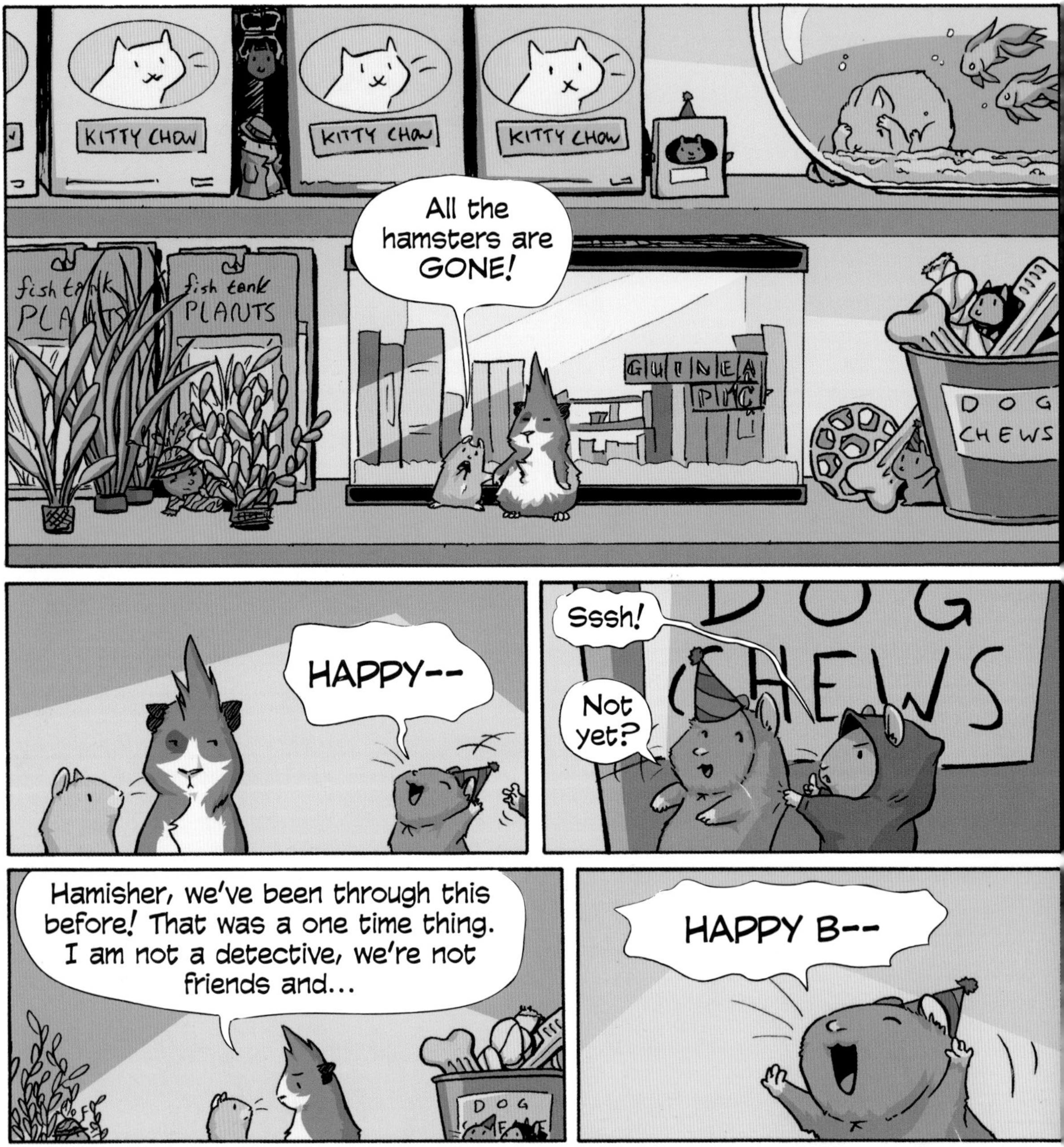
KITTY CHOW
KITTY CHOW
KITTY CHOW
fish tank PLANTS
fish tank PLANTS
All the hamsters are GONE!
GUINEA PIG
DOG CHEWS
HAPPY--
DOG CHEWS
Sssh!
Not yet?
Hamisher, we've been through this before! That was a one time thing. I am not a detective, we're not friends and...
HAPPY B--

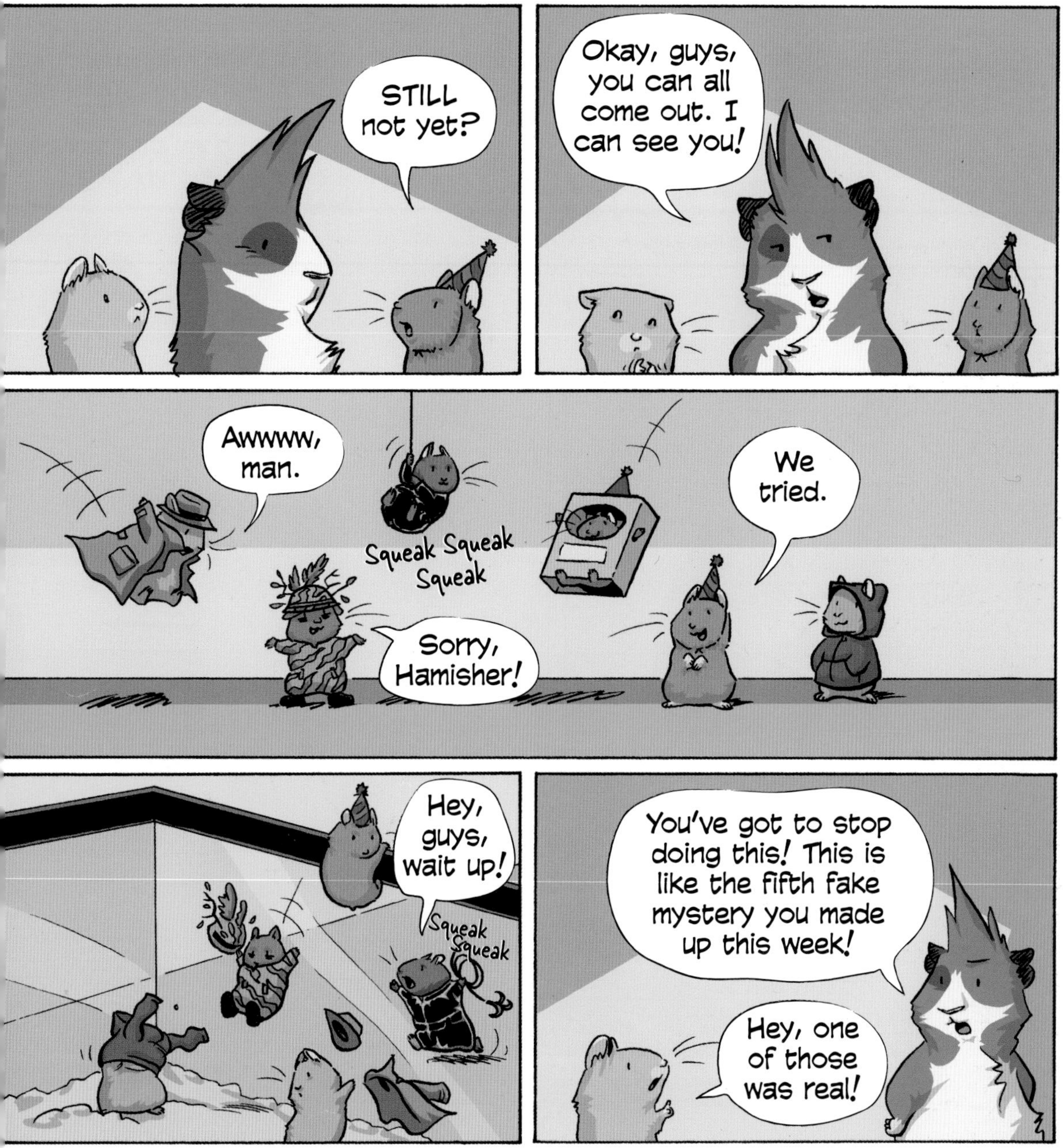
STILL not yet?
Okay, guys, you can all come out. I can see you!
Awwww, man.
Squeak Squeak Squeak
We tried.
Sorry, Hamisher!
Hey, guys, wait up!
Squeak Squeak
You've got to stop doing this! This is like the fifth fake mystery you made up this week!
Hey, one of those was real!

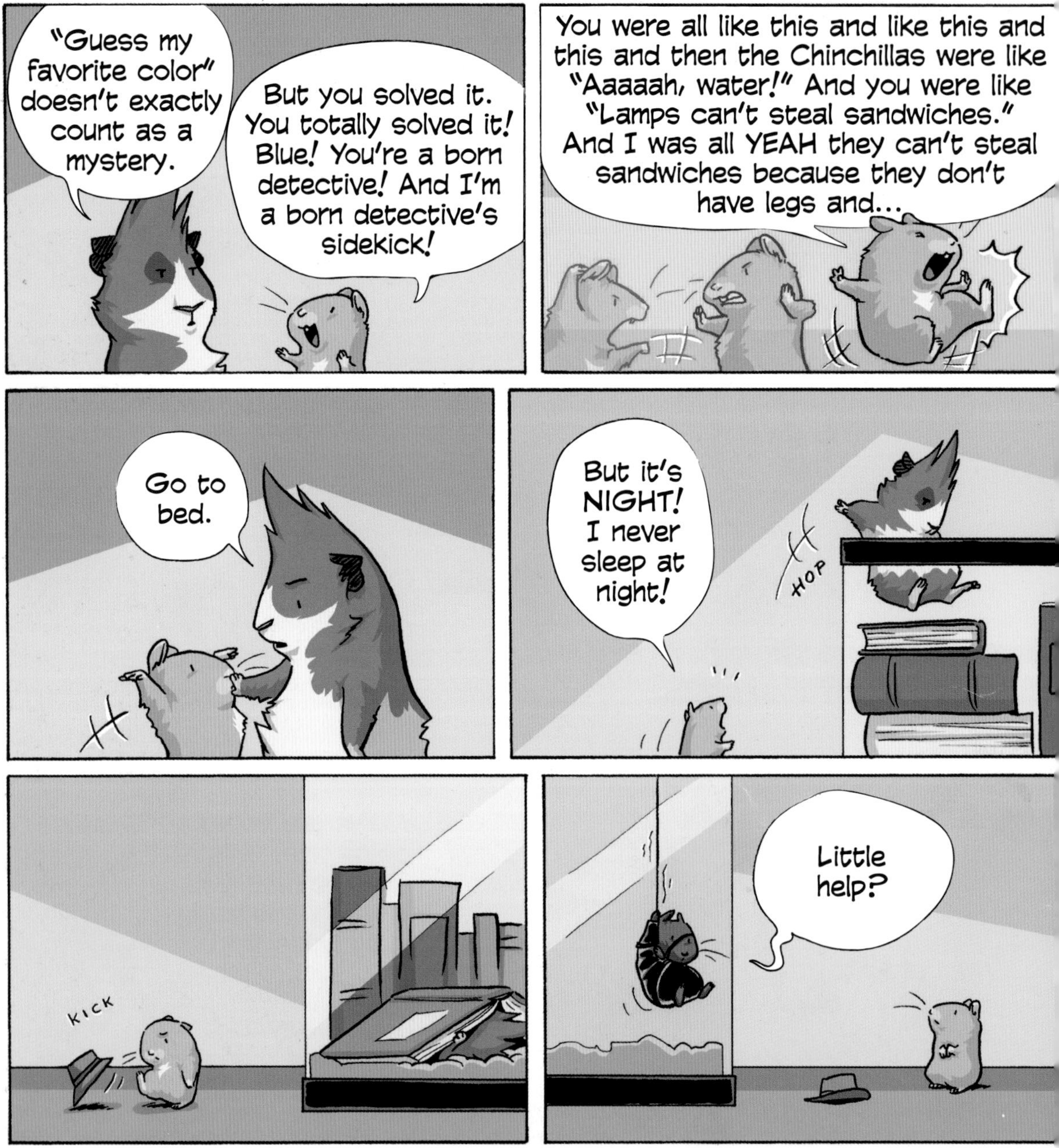
"Guess my favorite color" doesn't exactly count as a mystery.
But you solved it. You totally solved it! Blue! You're a born detective! And I'm a born detective's sidekick!
You were all like this and like this and this and then the Chinchillas were like "Aaaaah, water!" And you were like "Lamps can't steal sandwiches." And I was all YEAH they can't steal sandwiches because they don't have legs and...
Go to bed.
But it's NIGHT! I never sleep at night!
HOP
KICK
Little help?

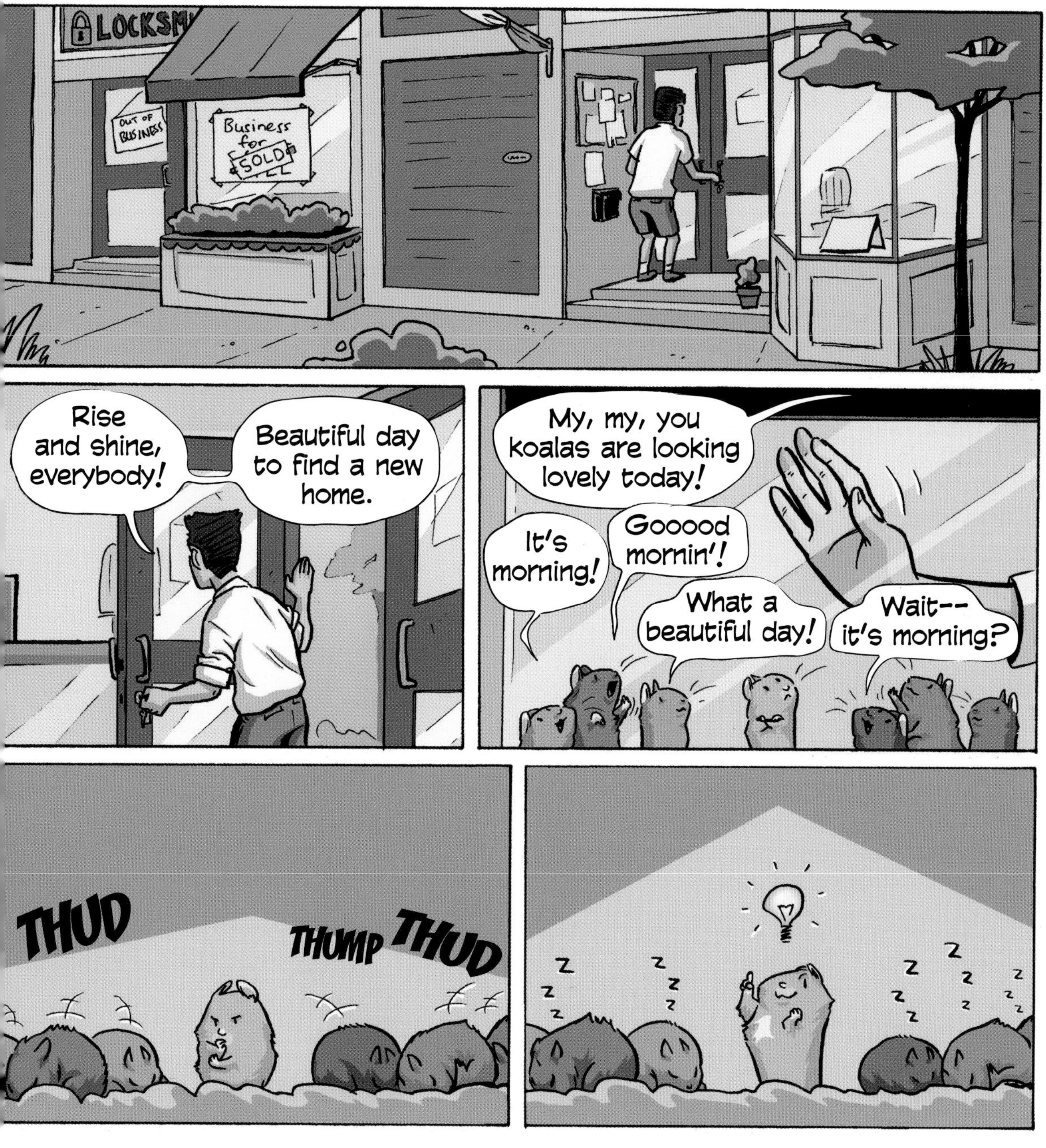
LOCKSM
OUT OF BUSINESS
Business for SALE
SOLD
Rise and shine, everybody!
Beautiful day to find a new home.
My, my, you koalas are looking lovely today!
It's morning!
Gooood mornin'!
What a beautiful day!
Wait-- it's morning?
THUD
THUMP
THUD
Z Z Z
Z Z Z
Z Z Z Z Z
Z Z Z

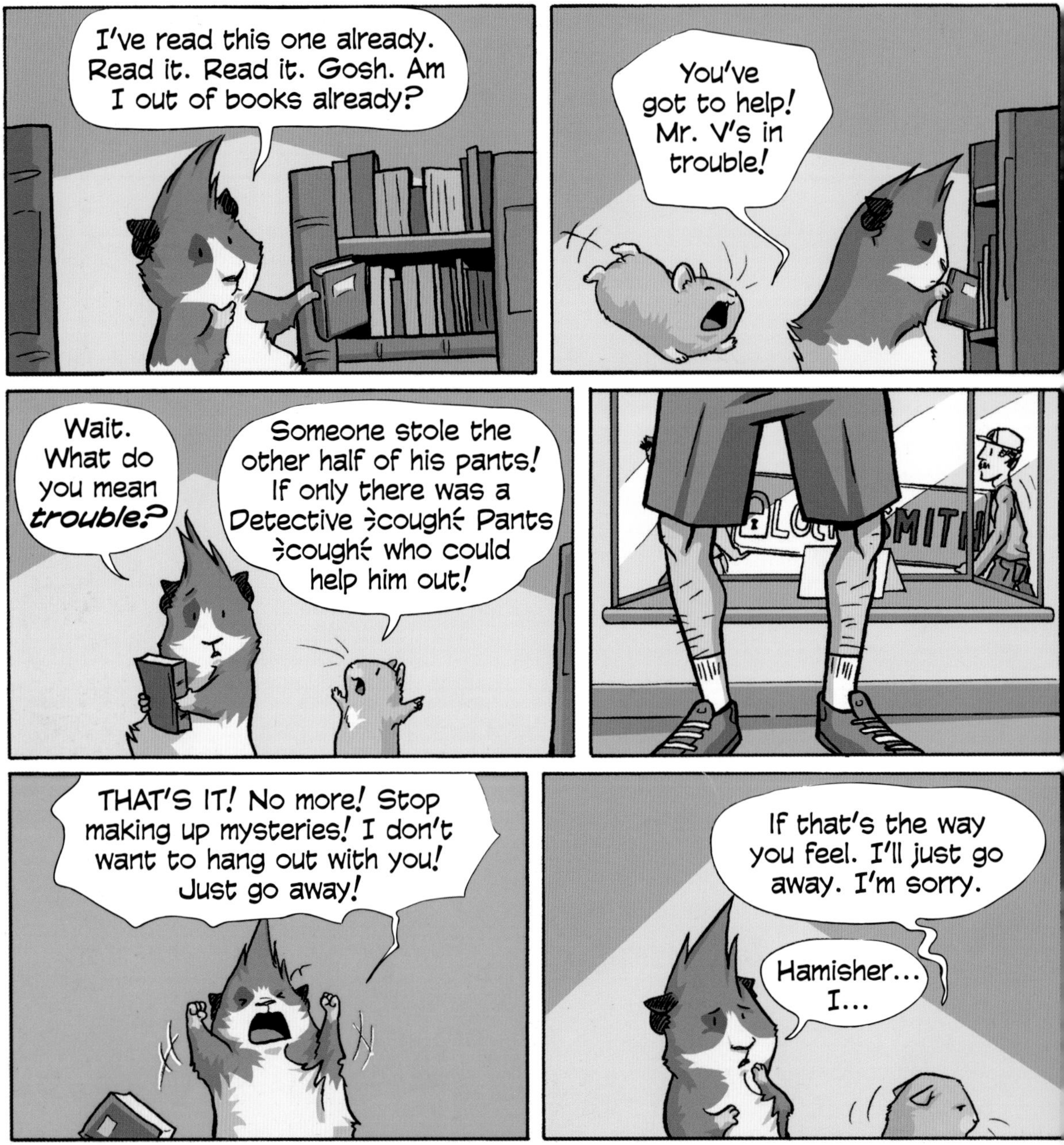
I've read this one already. Read it. Read it. Gosh. Am I out of books already?
You've got to help! Mr. V's in trouble!
Wait. What do you mean *trouble?*
Someone stole the other half of his pants! If only there was a Detective ⥽cough⥼ Pants ⥽cough⥼ who could help him out!
LOCKSMITH
THAT'S IT! No more! Stop making up mysteries! I don't want to hang out with you! Just go away!
If that's the way you feel. I'll just go away. I'm sorry.
Hamisher... I...

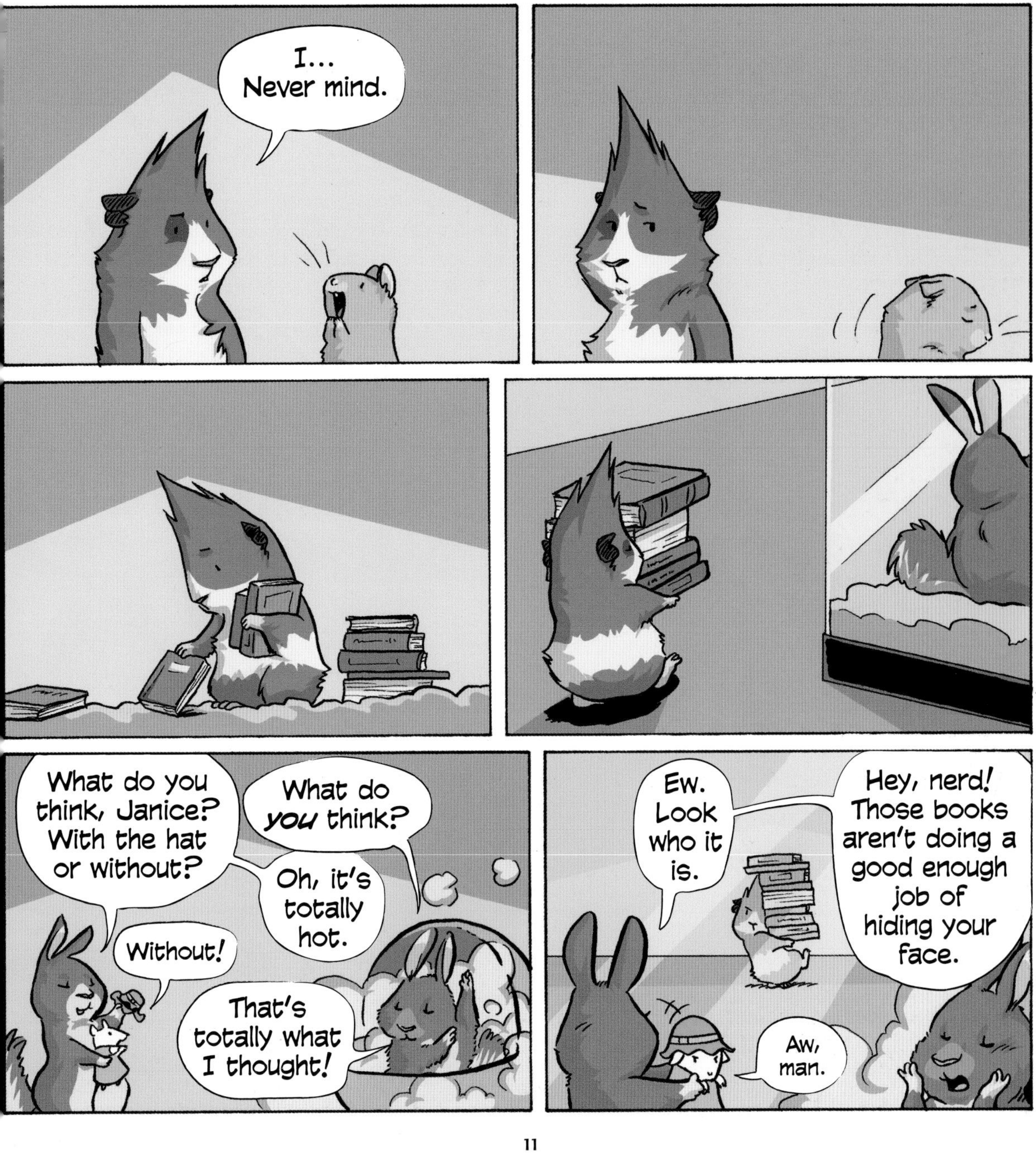
I... Never mind.
What do you think, Janice? With the hat or without?
What do ***you*** think?
Oh, it's totally hot.
Without!
That's totally what I thought!
Ew. Look who it is.
Hey, nerd! Those books aren't doing a good enough job of hiding your face.
Aw, man.

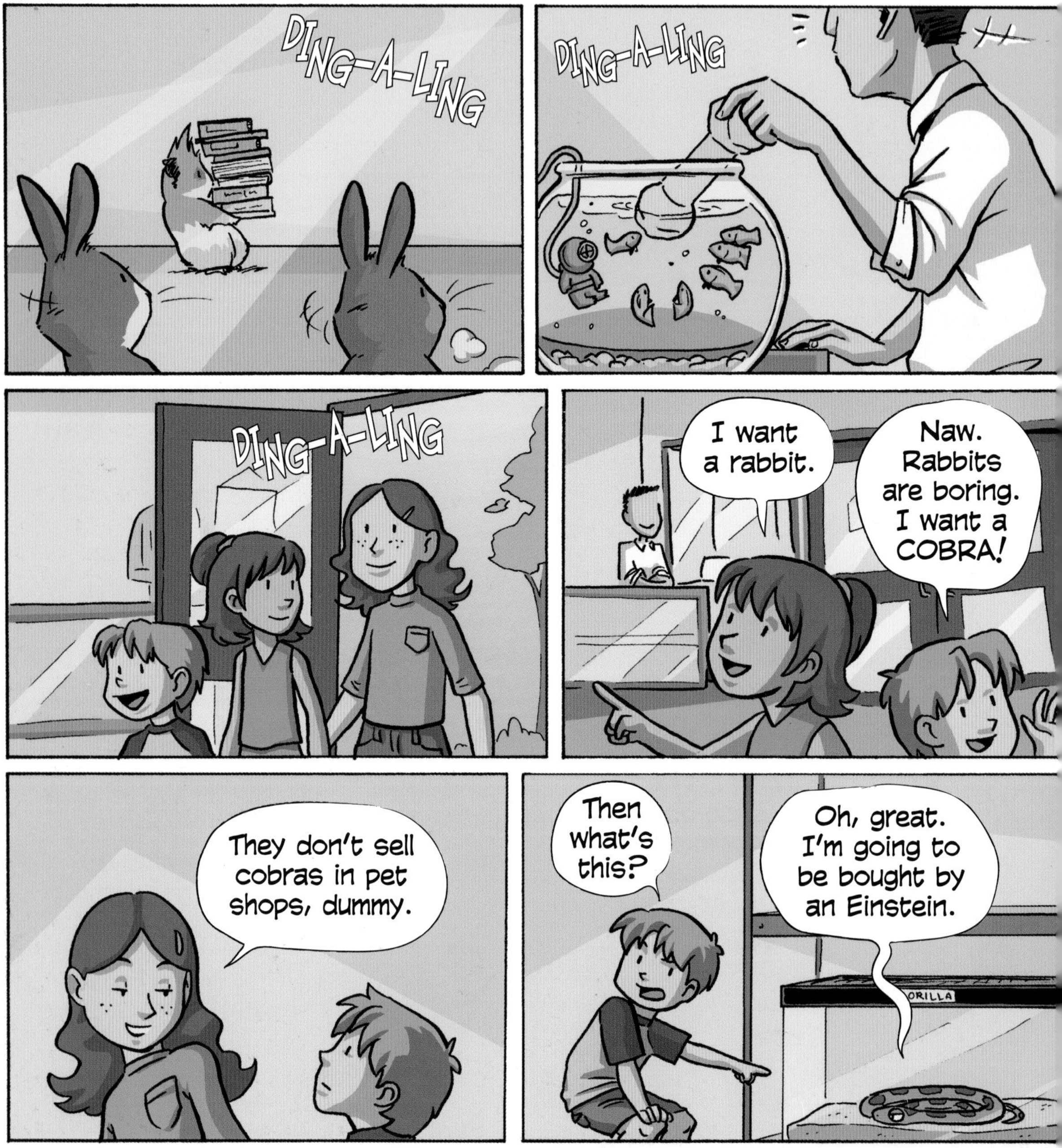
DING-A-LING
DING-A-LING
DING-A-LING
I want a rabbit.
Naw. Rabbits are boring. I want a COBRA!
They don't sell cobras in pet shops, dummy.
Then what's this?
Oh, great. I'm going to be bought by an Einstein.
ORILLA

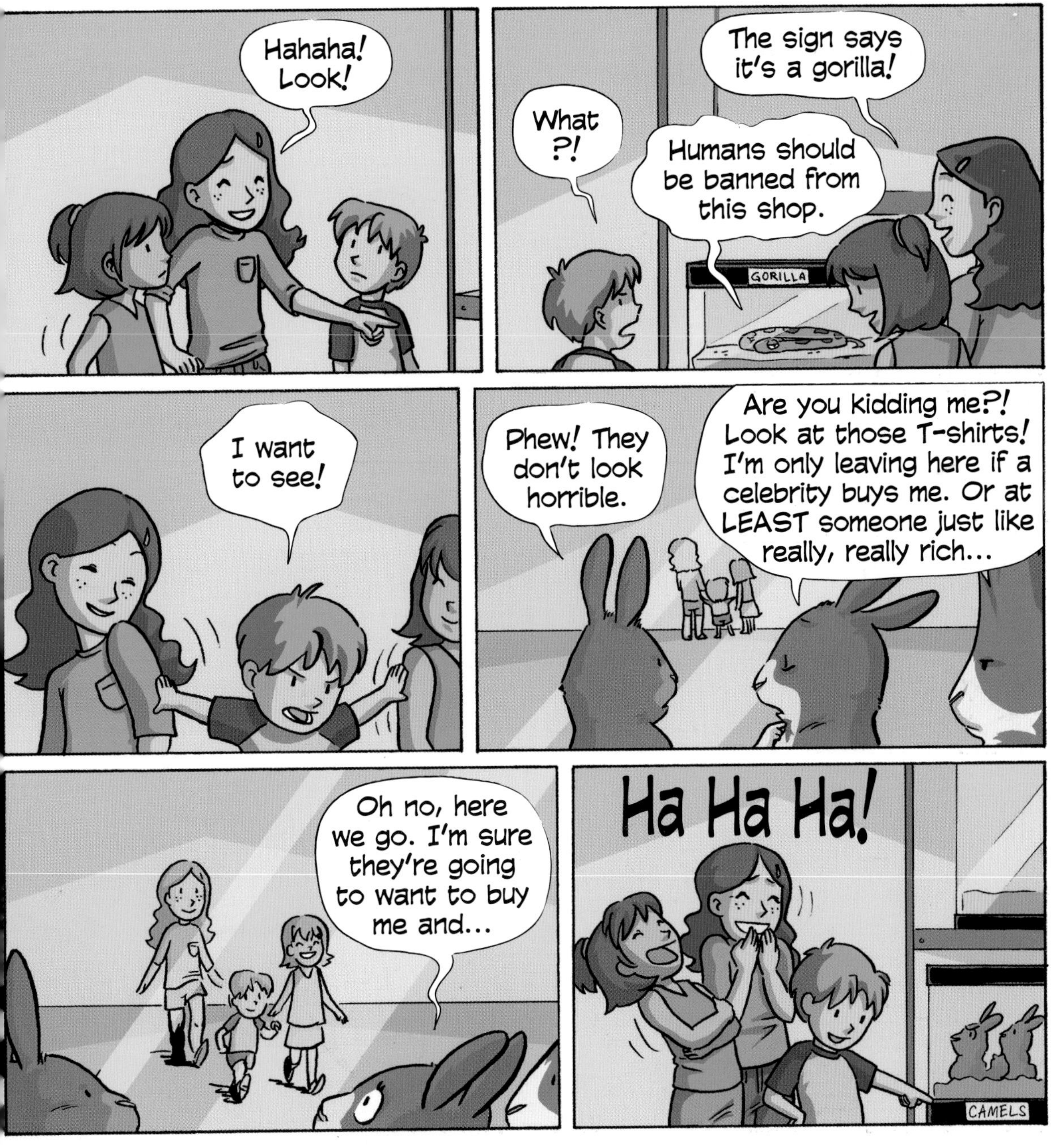
Hahaha! Look!
What ?!
The sign says it's a gorilla!
Humans should be banned from this shop.
GORILLA
I want to see!
Phew! They don't look horrible.
Are you kidding me?! Look at those T-shirts! I'm only leaving here if a celebrity buys me. Or at LEAST someone just like really, really rich...
Oh no, here we go. I'm sure they're going to want to buy me and...
Ha Ha Ha!
CAMELS

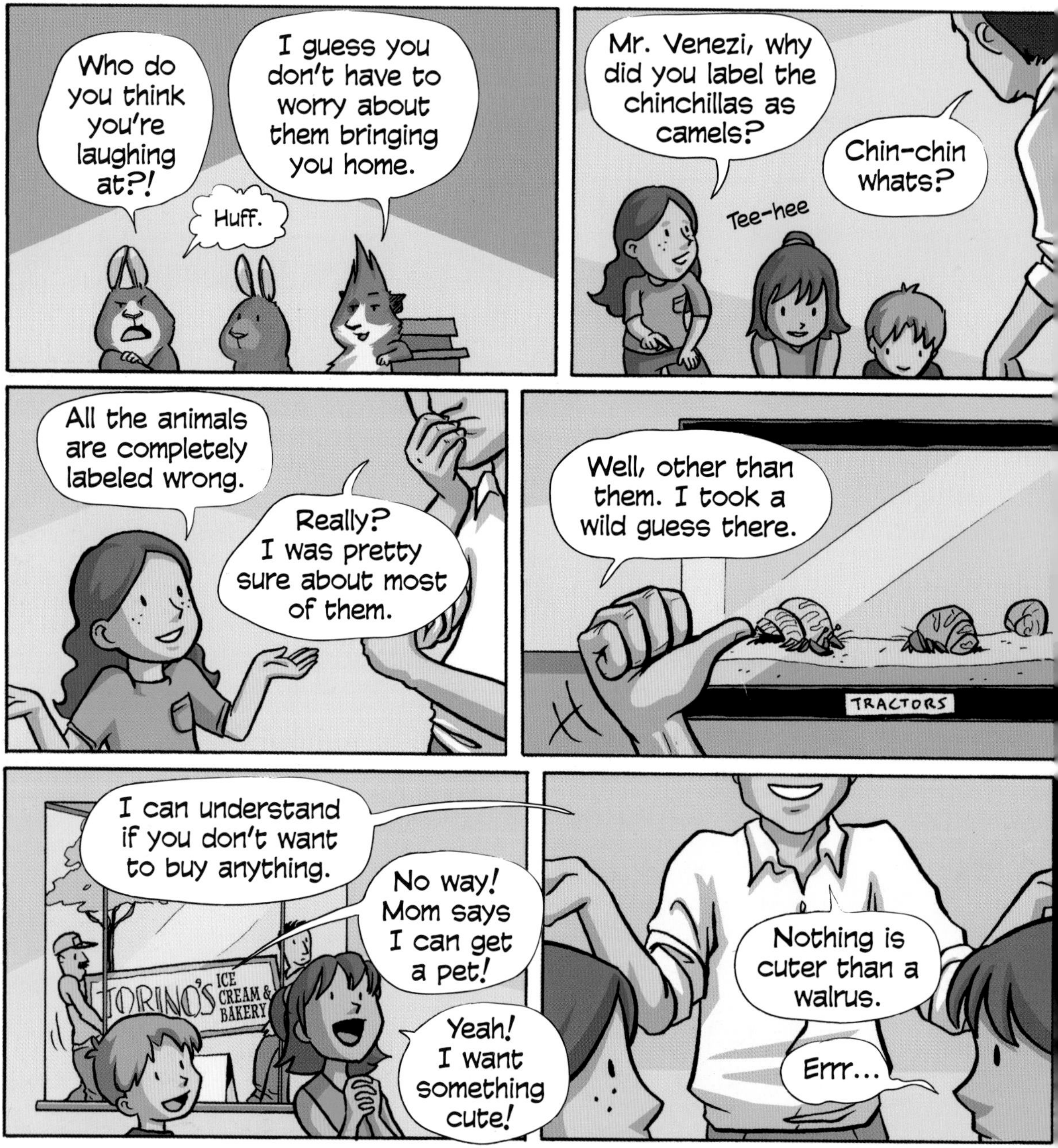

Who do you think you're laughing at?!
Huff.
I guess you don't have to worry about them bringing you home.
Mr. Venezi, why did you label the chinchillas as camels?
Tee-hee
Chin-chin whats?
All the animals are completely labeled wrong.
Really? I was pretty sure about most of them.
Well, other than them. I took a wild guess there.
TRACTORS
I can understand if you don't want to buy anything.
No way! Mom says I can get a pet!
TORINO'S ICE CREAM & BAKERY
Yeah! I want something cute!
Nothing is cuter than a walrus.
Errr...

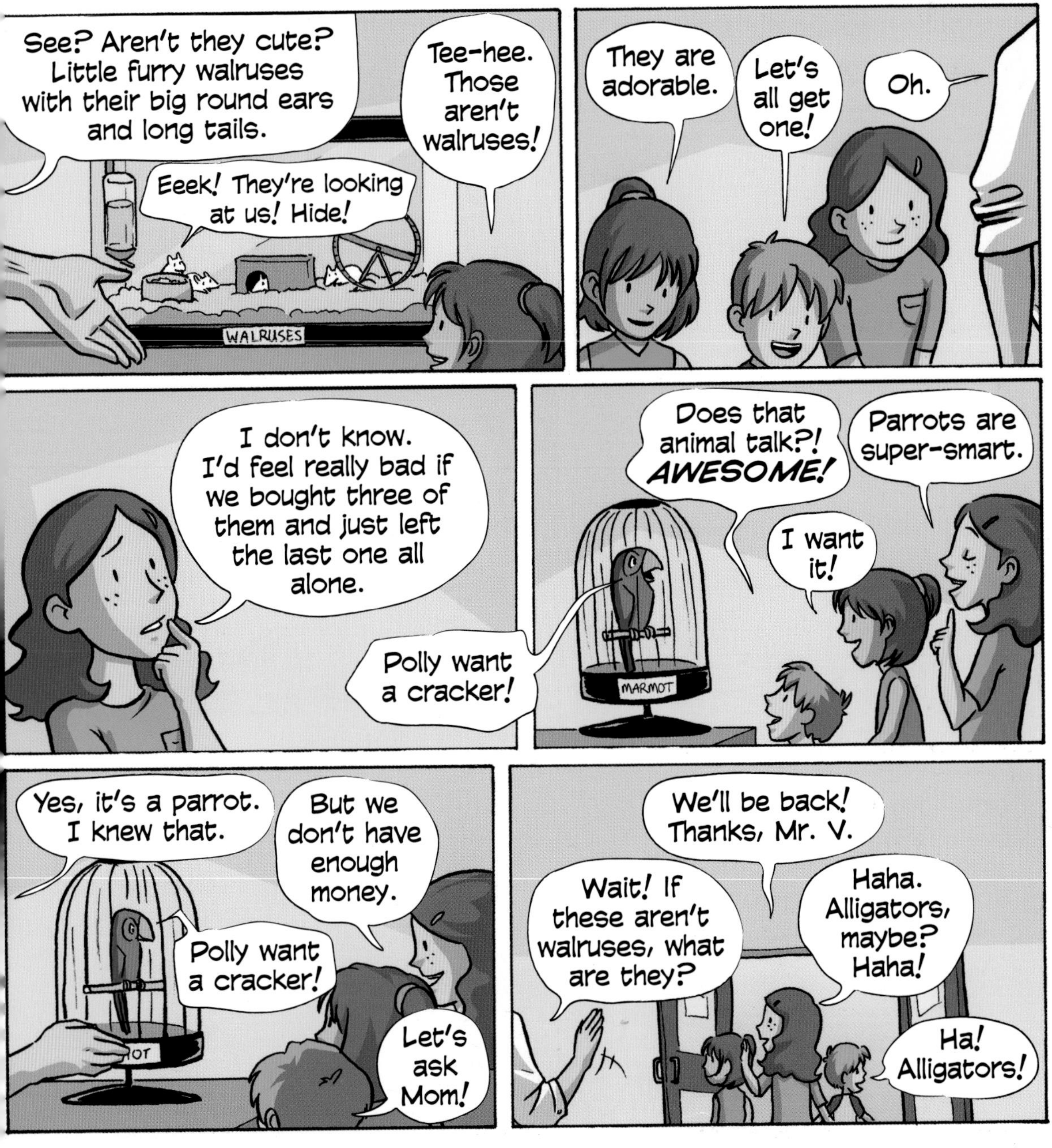
See? Aren't they cute? Little furry walruses with their big round ears and long tails.
Tee-hee. Those aren't walruses!
Eeek! They're looking at us! Hide!
WALRUSES
They are adorable.
Let's all get one!
Oh.
I don't know. I'd feel really bad if we bought three of them and just left the last one all alone.
Does that animal talk?! *AWESOME!*
Parrots are super-smart.
I want it!
Polly want a cracker!
MARMOT
Yes, it's a parrot. I knew that.
But we don't have enough money.
Polly want a cracker!
Let's ask Mom!
We'll be back! Thanks, Mr. V.
Wait! If these aren't walruses, what are they?
Haha. Alligators, maybe? Haha!
Ha! Alligators!

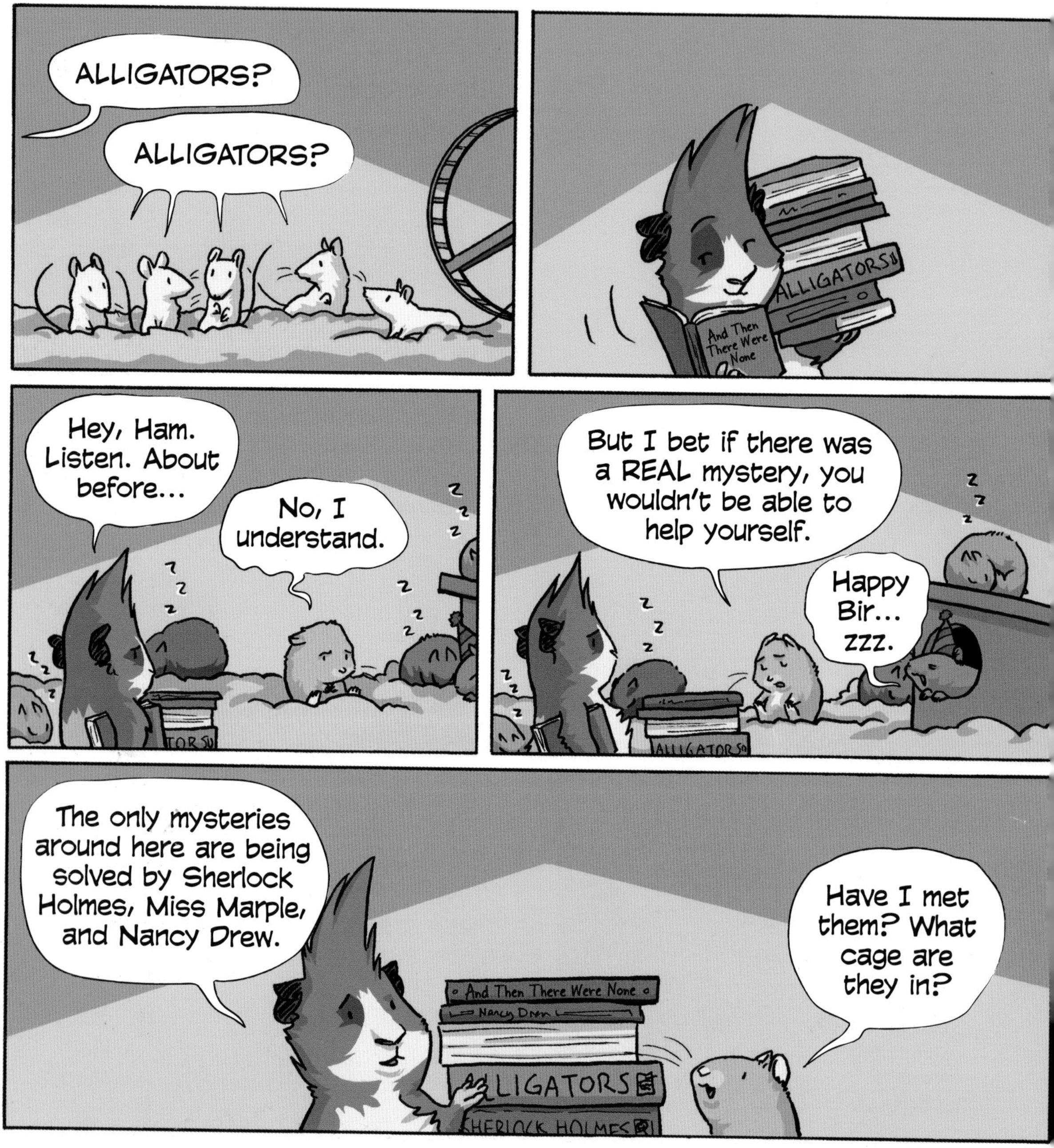
ALLIGATORS?
ALLIGATORS?
ALLIGATORS
And Then There Were None
Hey, Ham. Listen. About before...
No, I understand.
But I bet if there was a REAL mystery, you wouldn't be able to help yourself.
Happy Bir... zzz.
The only mysteries around here are being solved by Sherlock Holmes, Miss Marple, and Nancy Drew.
Have I met them? What cage are they in?
And Then There Were None
Nancy Drew
ALLIGATORS
SHERLOCK HOLMES

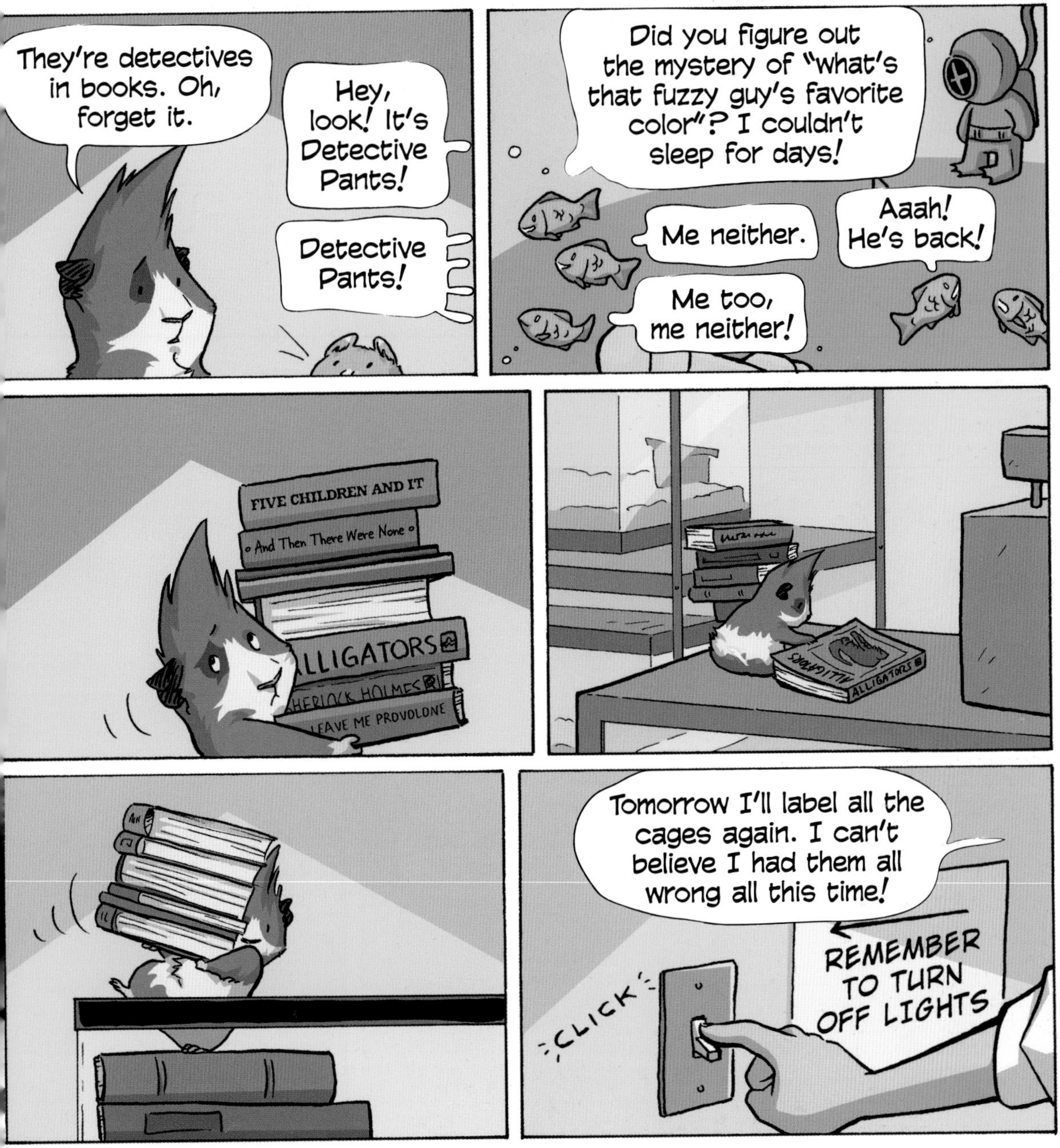
They're detectives in books. Oh, forget it.
Hey, look! It's Detective Pants!
Detective Pants!
Did you figure out the mystery of "what's that fuzzy guy's favorite color"? I couldn't sleep for days!
Me neither.
Aaah! He's back!
Me too, me neither!
FIVE CHILDREN AND IT
And Then There Were None
LLIGATORS
HERLOCK HOLMES
EAVE ME PROVOLONE
ALLIGATORS
Tomorrow I'll label all the cages again. I can't believe I had them all wrong all this time!
REMEMBER TO TURN OFF LIGHTS
CLICK

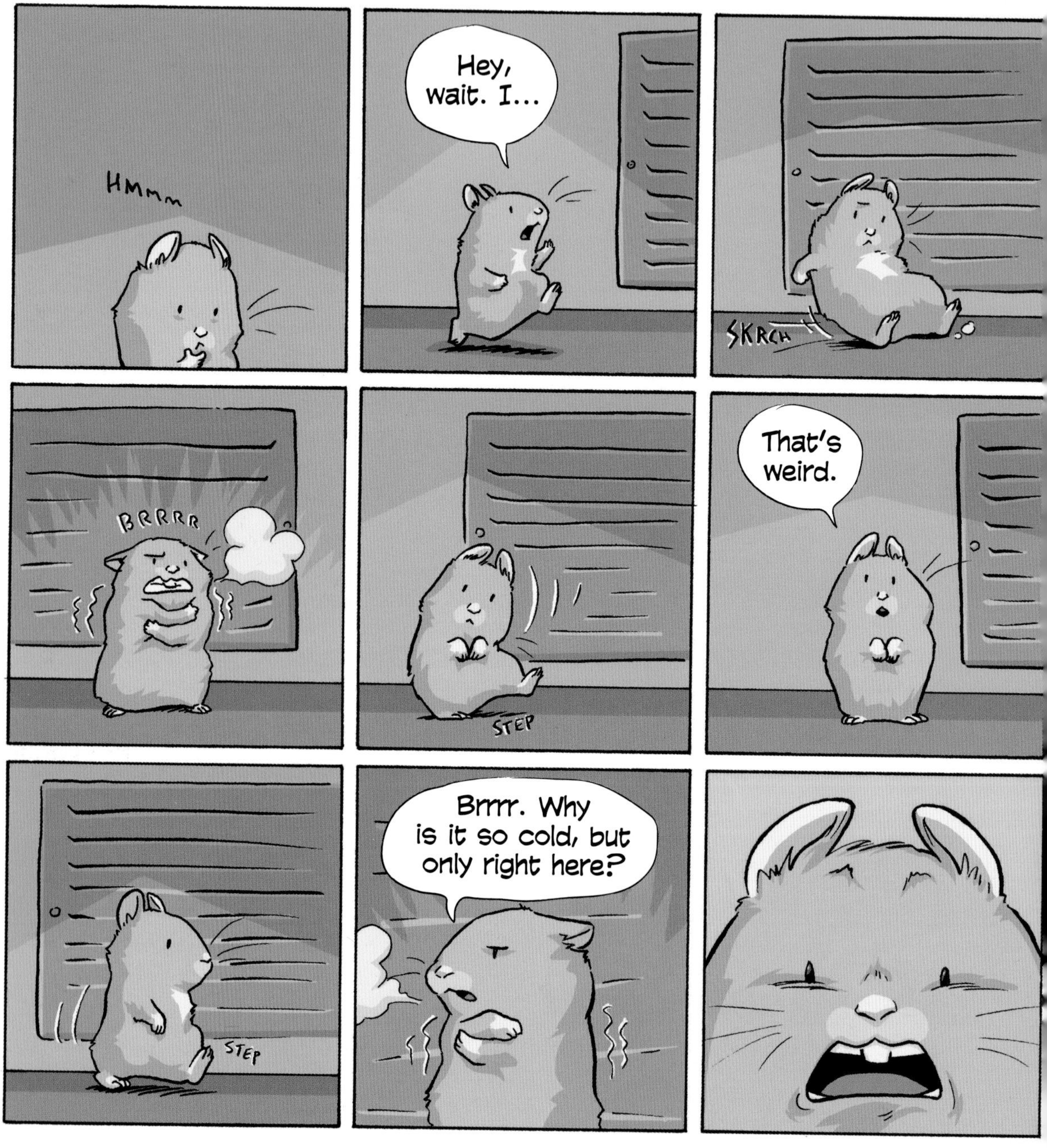
HMMM
Hey, wait. I...
SKRCH
BRRRR
STEP
That's weird.
STEP
Brrrr. Why is it so cold, but only right here?

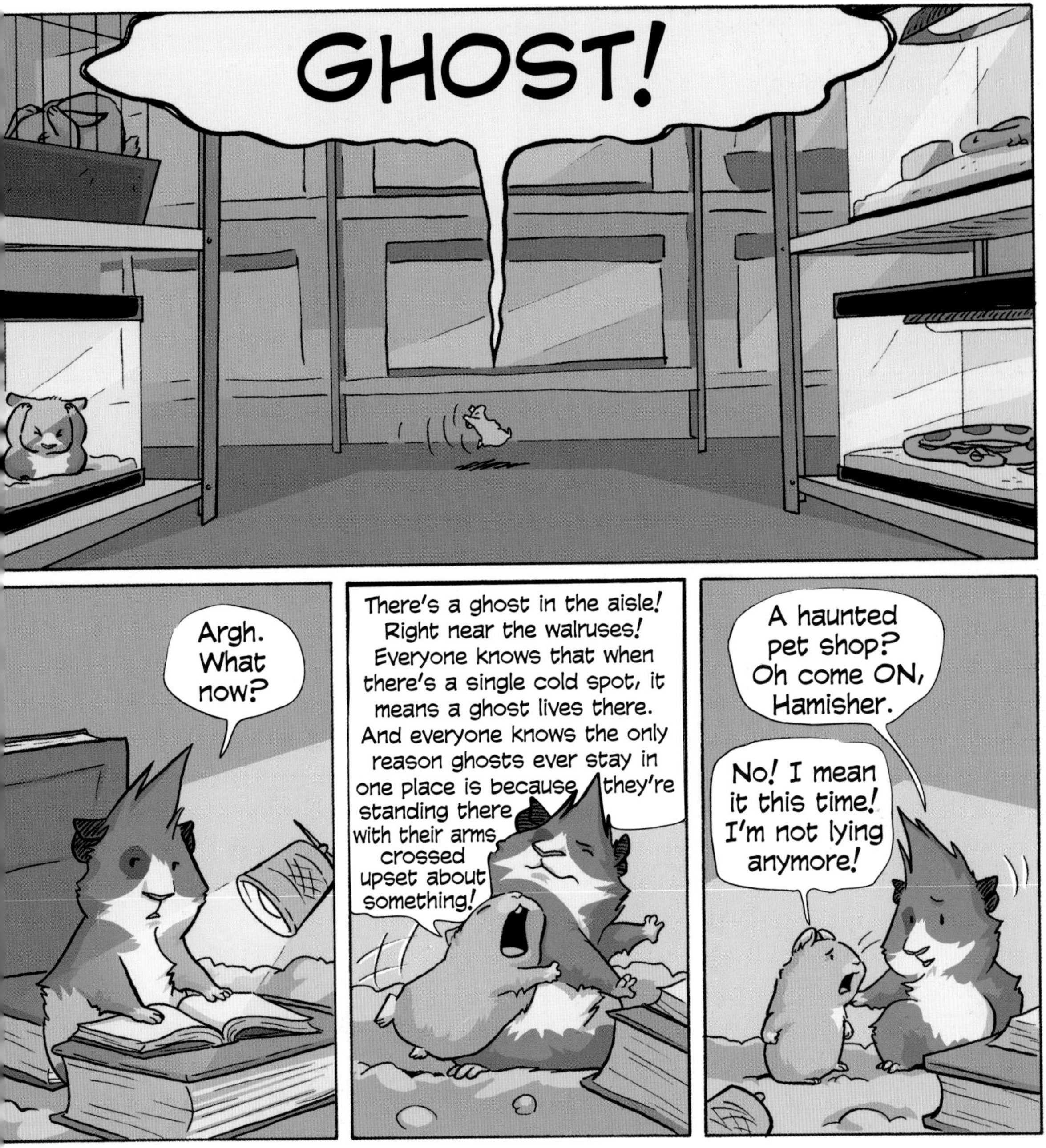
GHOST!
Argh. What now?
There's a ghost in the aisle! Right near the walruses! Everyone knows that when there's a single cold spot, it means a ghost lives there. And everyone knows the only reason ghosts ever stay in one place is because they're standing there with their arms crossed upset about something!
A haunted pet shop? Oh come ON, Hamisher.
No! I mean it this time! I'm not lying anymore!

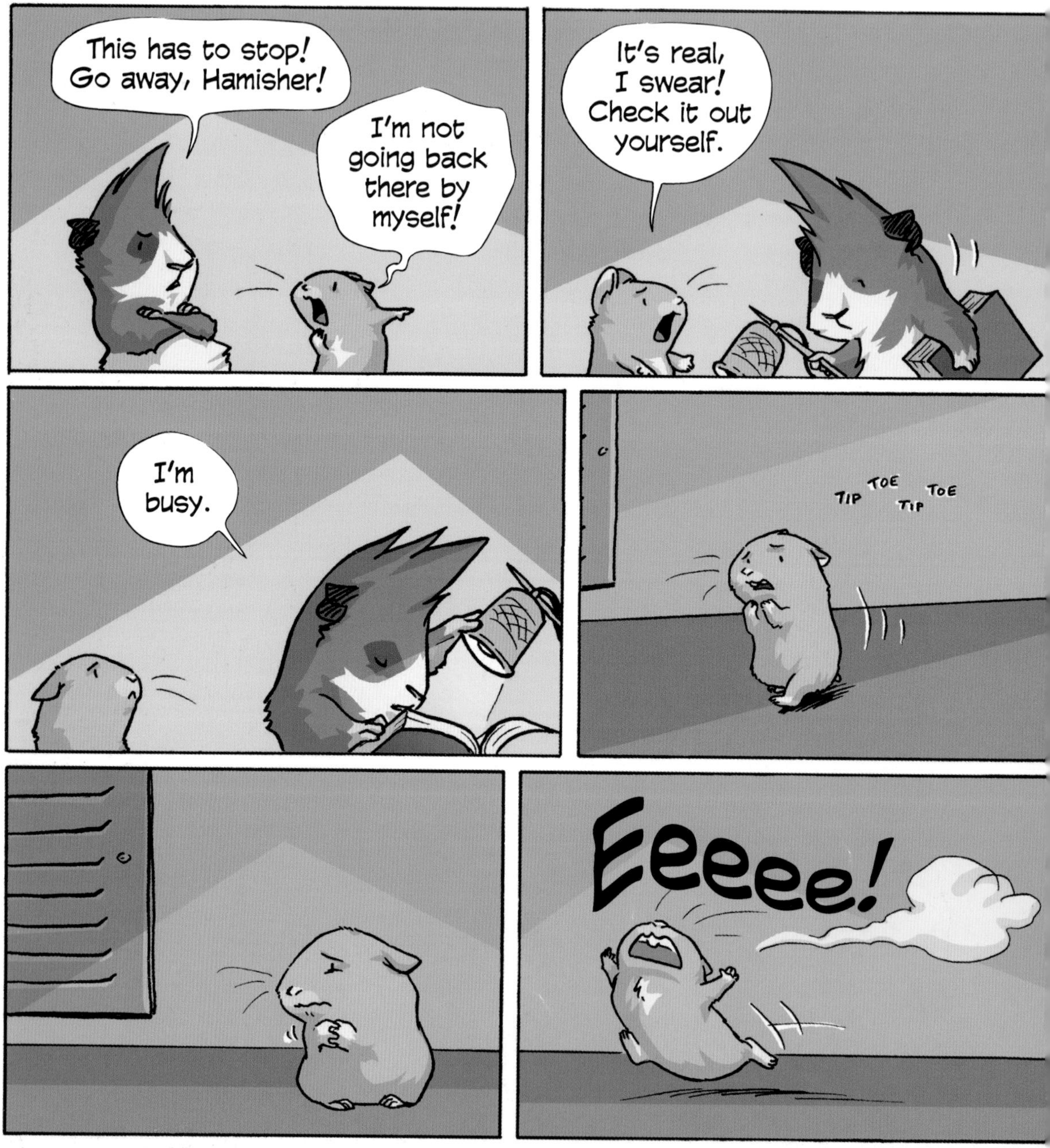
This has to stop! Go away, Hamisher!
I'm not going back there by myself!
It's real, I swear! Check it out yourself.
I'm busy.
TIP TOE TIP TOE
Eeeee!

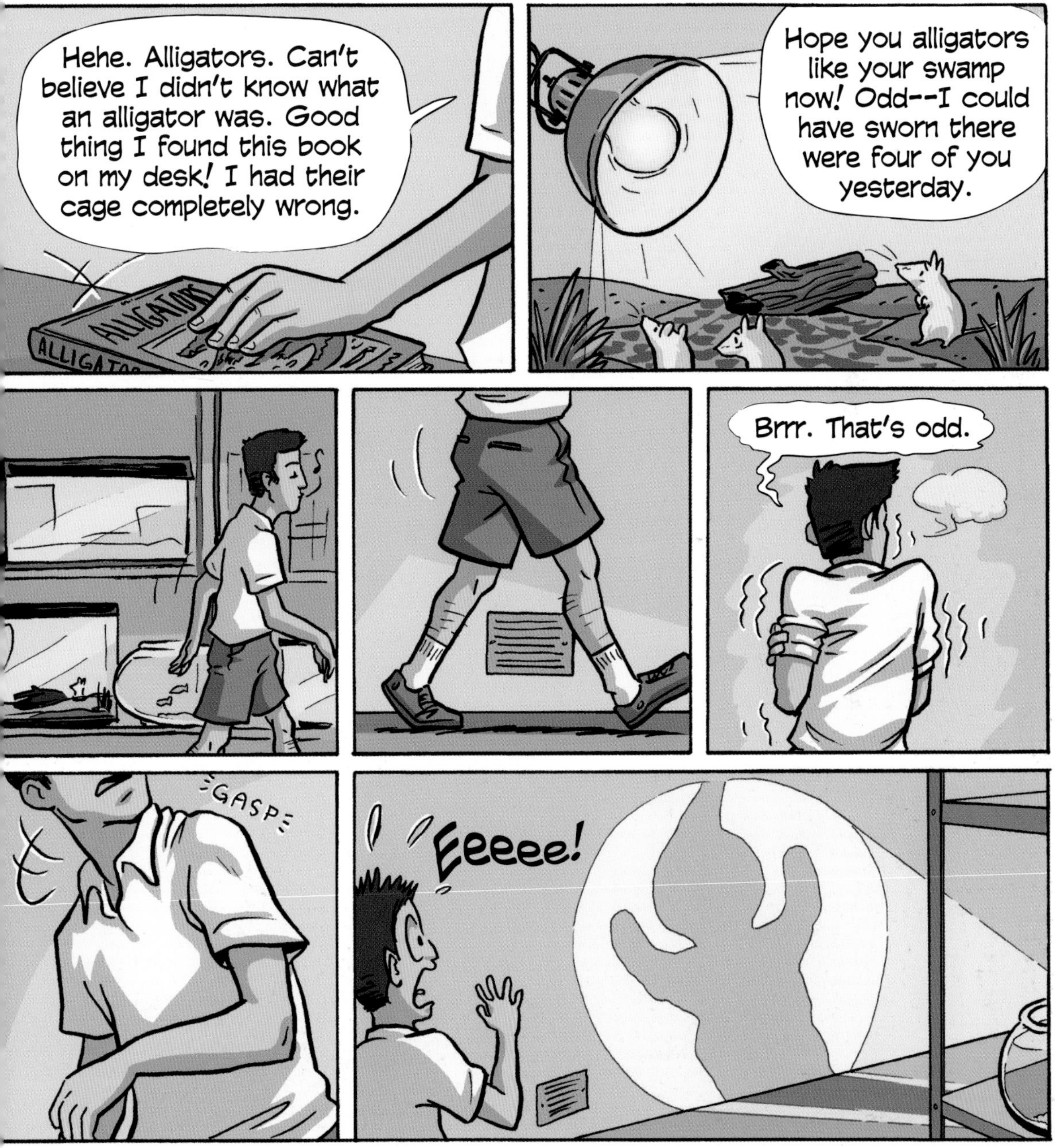
Hehe. Alligators. Can't believe I didn't know what an alligator was. Good thing I found this book on my desk! I had their cage completely wrong.
ALLIGATORS
Hope you alligators like your swamp now! Odd--I could have sworn there were four of you yesterday.
Brrr. That's odd.
GASP
Eeeee!

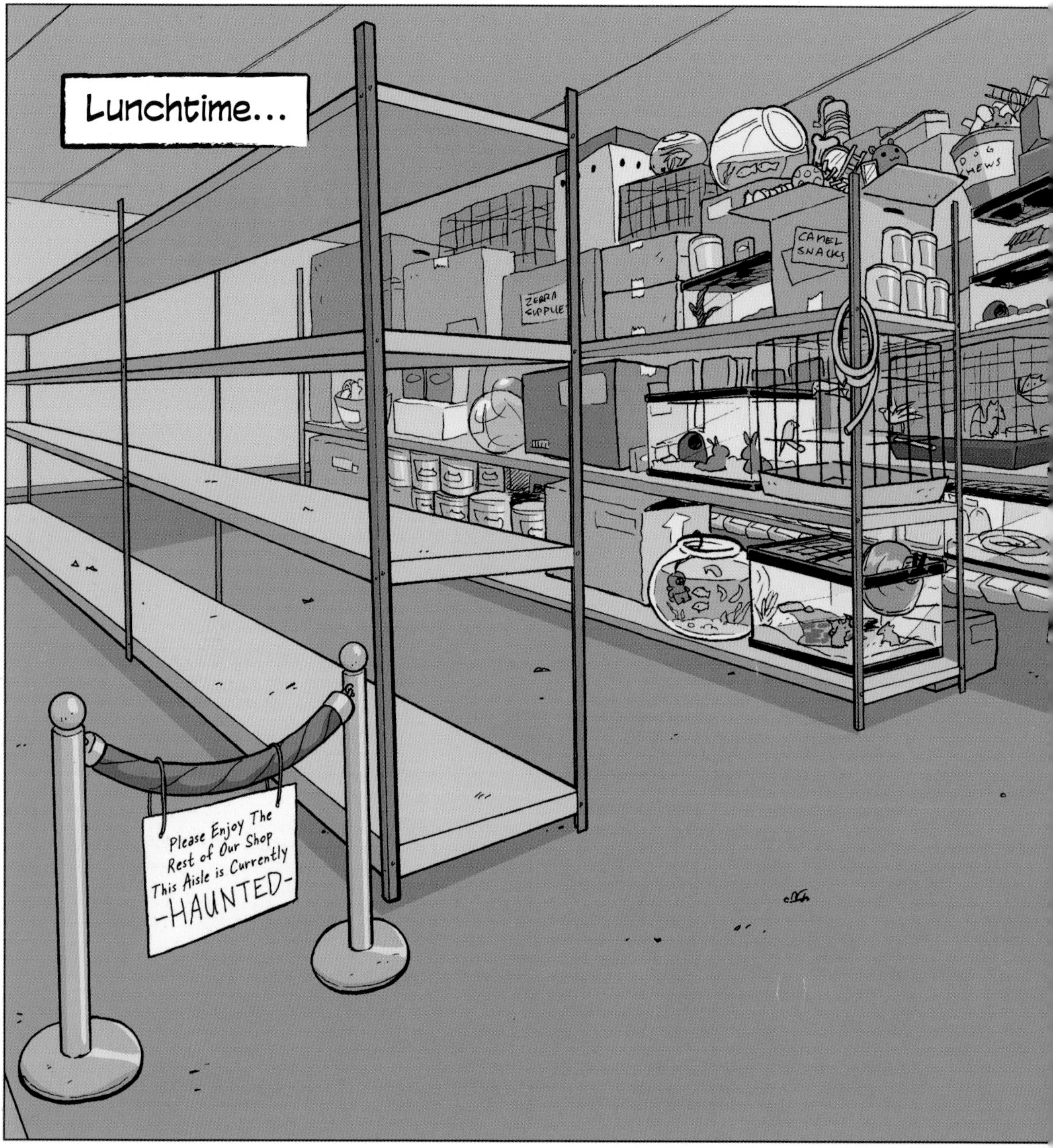
Lunchtime...
ZEBRA SUPPLIES
CAMEL SNACKS
DOG CHEWS
Please Enjoy The Rest of Our Shop
This Aisle is Currently
-HAUNTED-

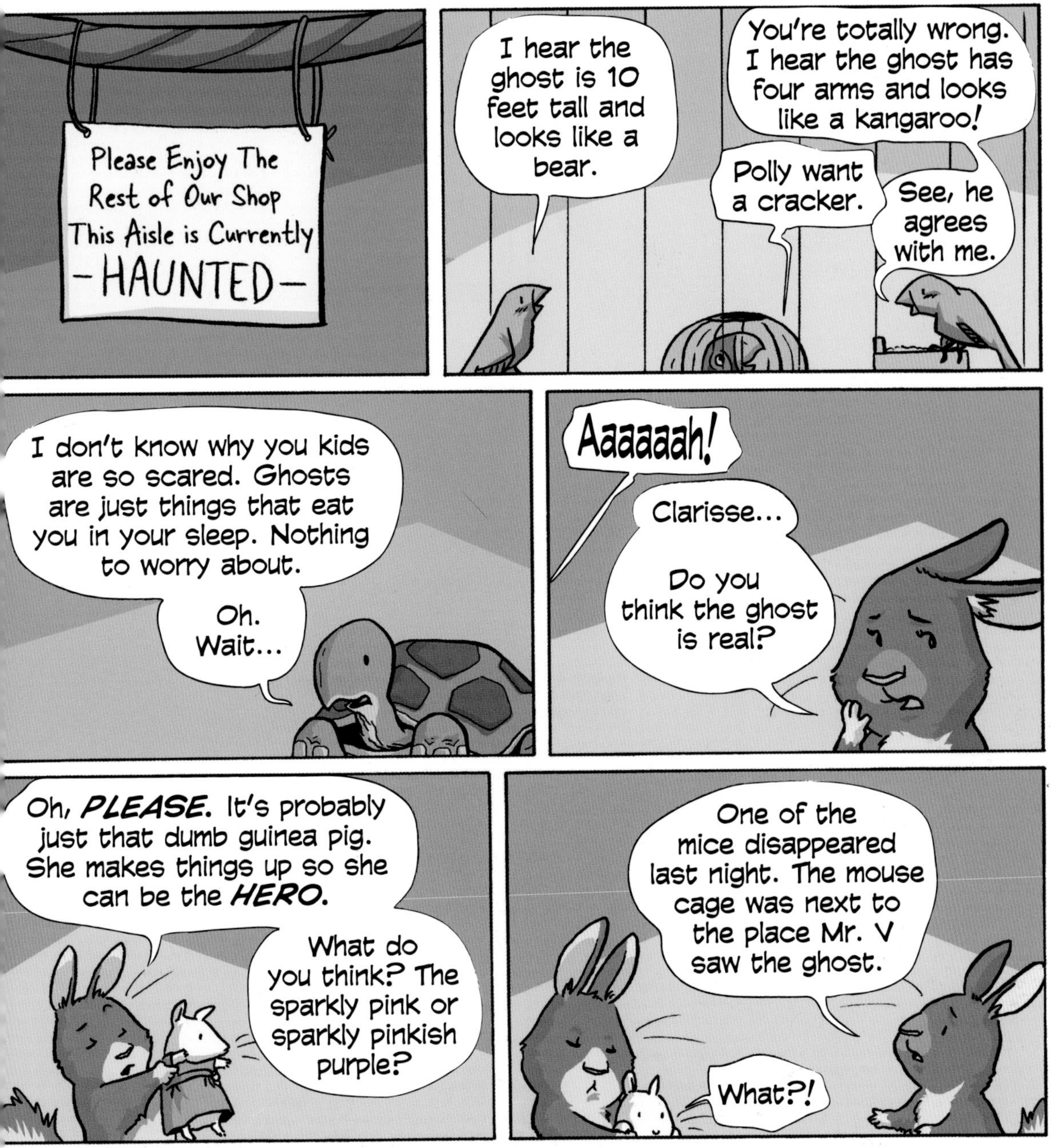
Please Enjoy The Rest of Our Shop This Aisle is Currently -HAUNTED-
I hear the ghost is 10 feet tall and looks like a bear.
You're totally wrong. I hear the ghost has four arms and looks like a kangaroo!
Polly want a cracker.
See, he agrees with me.
I don't know why you kids are so scared. Ghosts are just things that eat you in your sleep. Nothing to worry about.
Oh. Wait...
Aaaaaah!
Clarisse...
Do you think the ghost is real?
Oh, *PLEASE.* It's probably just that dumb guinea pig. She makes things up so she can be the *HERO.*
What do you think? The sparkly pink or sparkly pinkish purple?
One of the mice disappeared last night. The mouse cage was next to the place Mr. V saw the ghost.
What?!

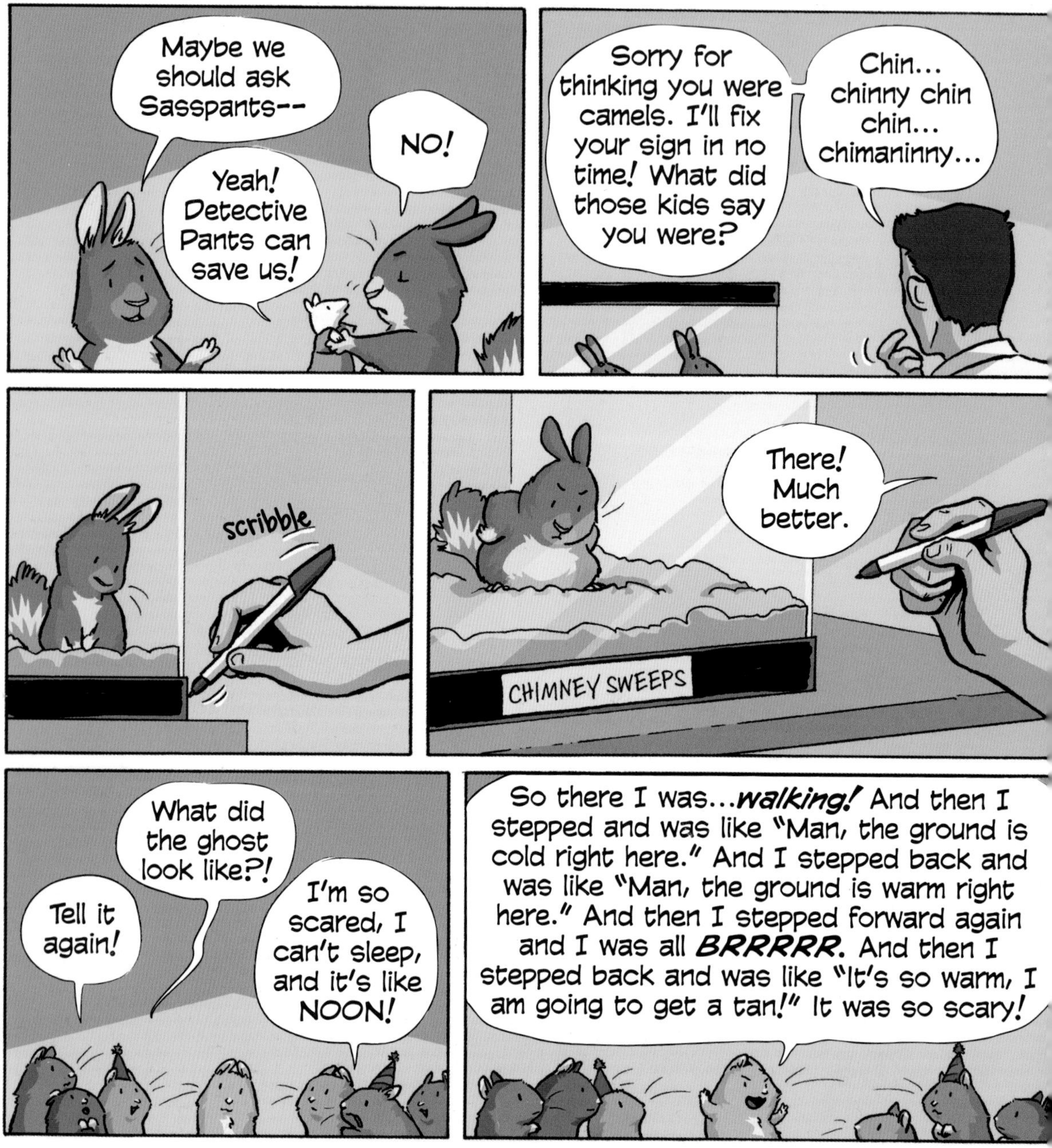
Maybe we should ask Sasspants--
Yeah! Detective Pants can save us!
NO!
Sorry for thinking you were camels. I'll fix your sign in no time! What did those kids say you were?
Chin... chinny chin chin... chimaninny...
scribble
There! Much better.
CHIMNEY SWEEPS
Tell it again!
What did the ghost look like?!
I'm so scared, I can't sleep, and it's like NOON!
So there I was...walking! And then I stepped and was like "Man, the ground is cold right here." And I stepped back and was like "Man, the ground is warm right here." And then I stepped forward again and I was all BRRRRR. And then I stepped back and was like "It's so warm, I am going to get a tan!" It was so scary!

So scary!

So brave!

So how is Detective Pants going to catch the ghost?

She doesn't believe me.

What?!

No way!

But you got cold and then hot and then cold and then hot, and Mr. V saw it!

She thinks I'm making it up!

Are you?

Sorry, ghost! Just passing through!

Hmmm, let's see. No tails. Check! A little fuzzy. Check! Pointy hats. Check!

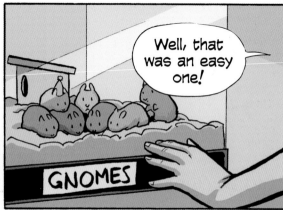

Well, that was an easy one!

GNOMES

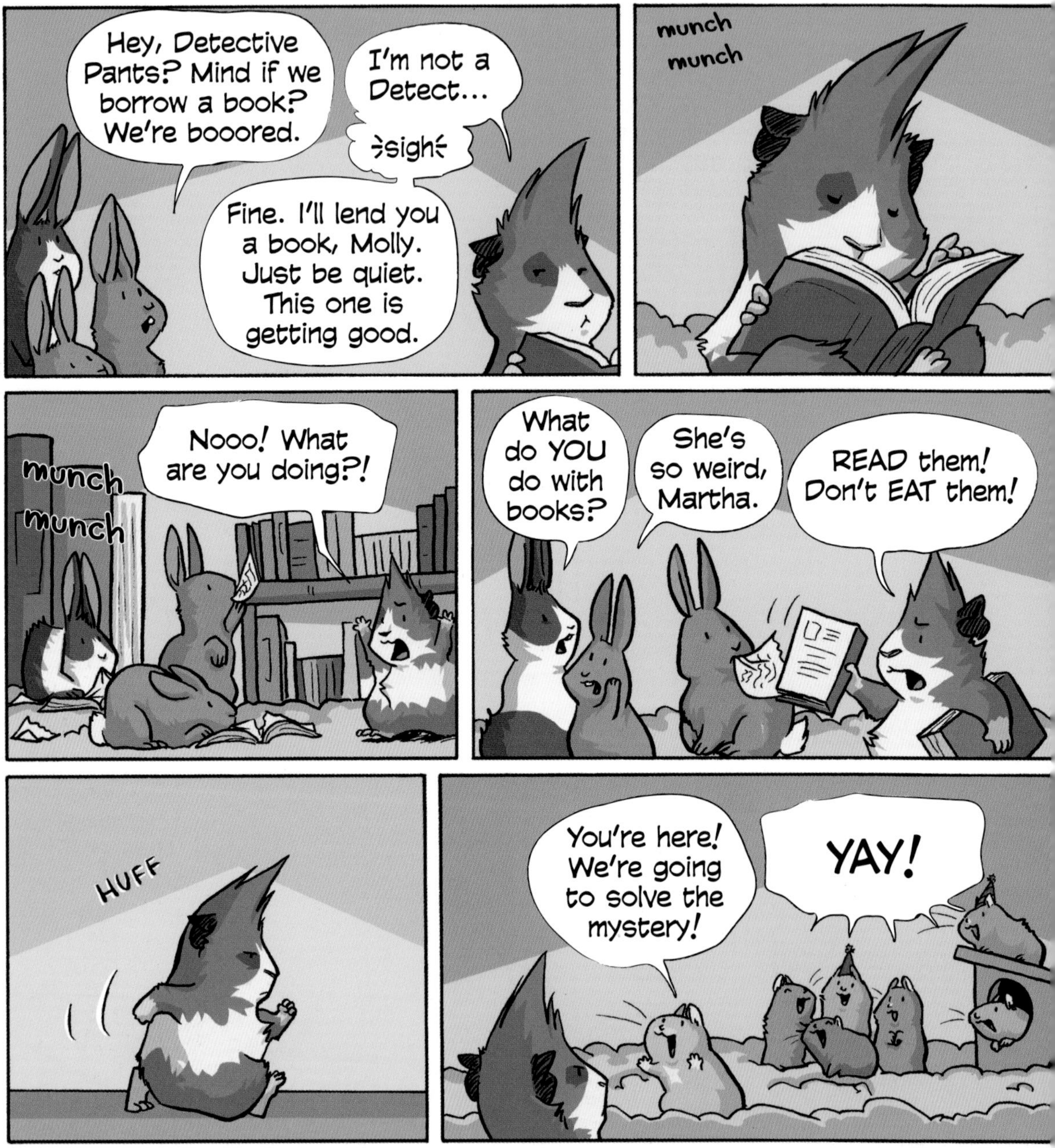
Hey, Detective Pants? Mind if we borrow a book? We're booored.
I'm not a Detect...
sigh
Fine. I'll lend you a book, Molly. Just be quiet. This one is getting good.
munch
munch
munch
munch
Nooo! What are you doing?!
What do YOU do with books?
She's so weird, Martha.
READ them! Don't EAT them!
HUFF
You're here! We're going to solve the mystery!
YAY!

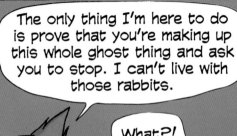

The only thing I'm here to do is prove that you're making up this whole ghost thing and ask you to stop. I can't live with those rabbits.

What?!

It's kinda obvious, Ham. You've been wanting to "solve a mystery" for weeks. It seems pretty convenient you were the one to uncover one.

I didn't do it! I swear there's a ghost!

Tell the truth.

I am! Cross my heart and eyes and legs and arms!

If you aren't going to confess, I guess I'll have to play detective one last time.

Oooh! Can I be your assistant?!

I probably don't have a choice, do I? Even though I am just doing this to prove you made it all up.

Nope, no choice!

Okay. We should start with some witnesses.

To the fish!

Well, they aren't smart enough to lie. I guess we could ask them first.

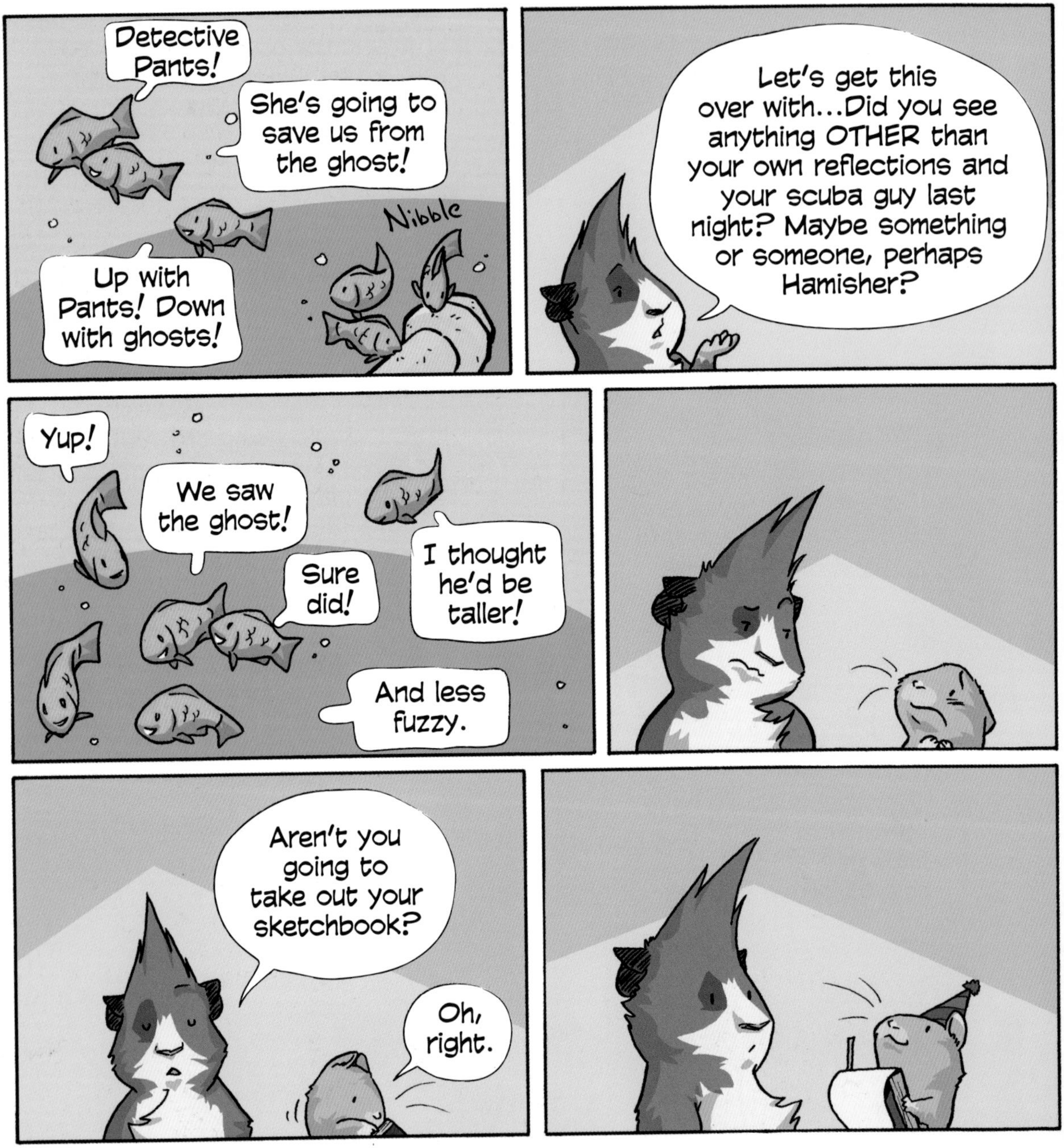
Detective Pants!
She's going to save us from the ghost!
Nibble
Up with Pants! Down with ghosts!
Let's get this over with...Did you see anything OTHER than your own reflections and your scuba guy last night? Maybe something or someone, perhaps Hamisher?
Yup!
We saw the ghost!
Sure did!
I thought he'd be taller!
And less fuzzy.
Aren't you going to take out your sketchbook?
Oh, right.

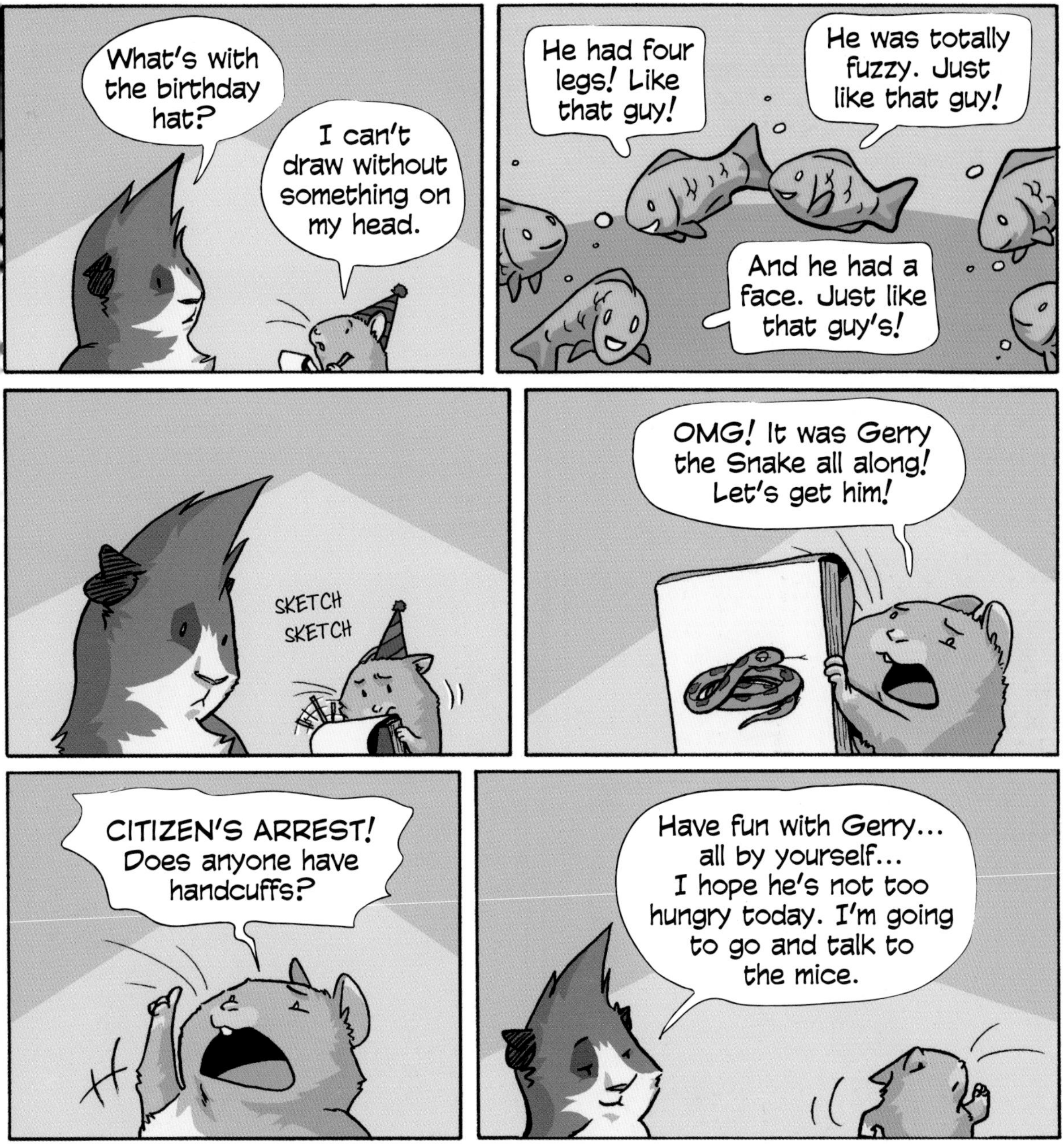
What's with the birthday hat?
I can't draw without something on my head.
He had four legs! Like that guy!
He was totally fuzzy. Just like that guy!
And he had a face. Just like that guy's!
SKETCH SKETCH
OMG! It was Gerry the Snake all along! Let's get him!
CITIZEN'S ARREST! Does anyone have handcuffs?
Have fun with Gerry... all by yourself... I hope he's not too hungry today. I'm going to go and talk to the mice.

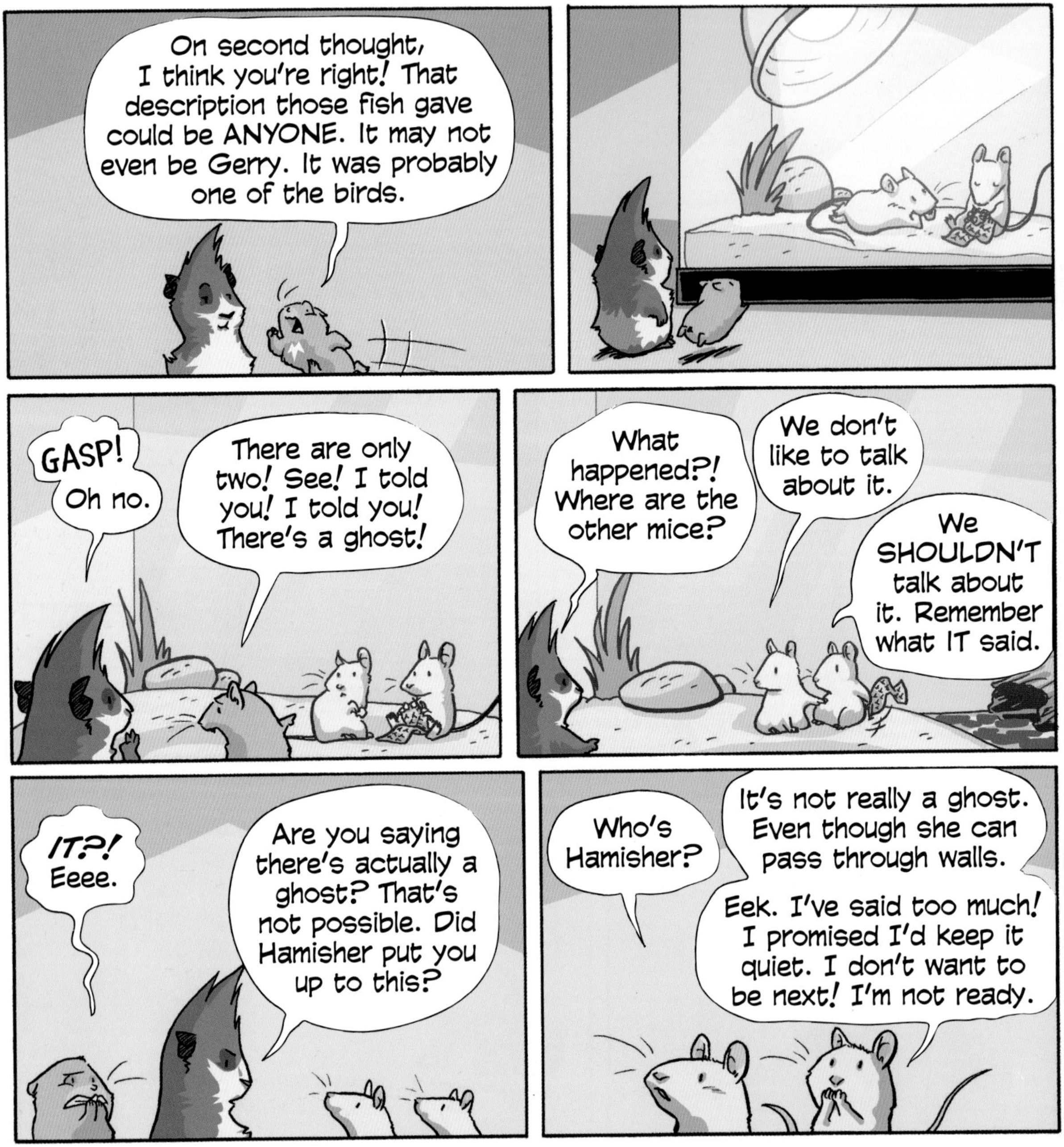
On second thought, I think you're right! That description those fish gave could be ANYONE. It may not even be Gerry. It was probably one of the birds.
GASP!
Oh no.
There are only two! See! I told you! I told you! There's a ghost!
What happened?! Where are the other mice?
We don't like to talk about it.
We SHOULDN'T talk about it. Remember what IT said.
IT?! Eeee.
Are you saying there's actually a ghost? That's not possible. Did Hamisher put you up to this?
Who's Hamisher?
It's not really a ghost. Even though she can pass through walls.
Eek. I've said too much! I promised I'd keep it quiet. I don't want to be next! I'm not ready.

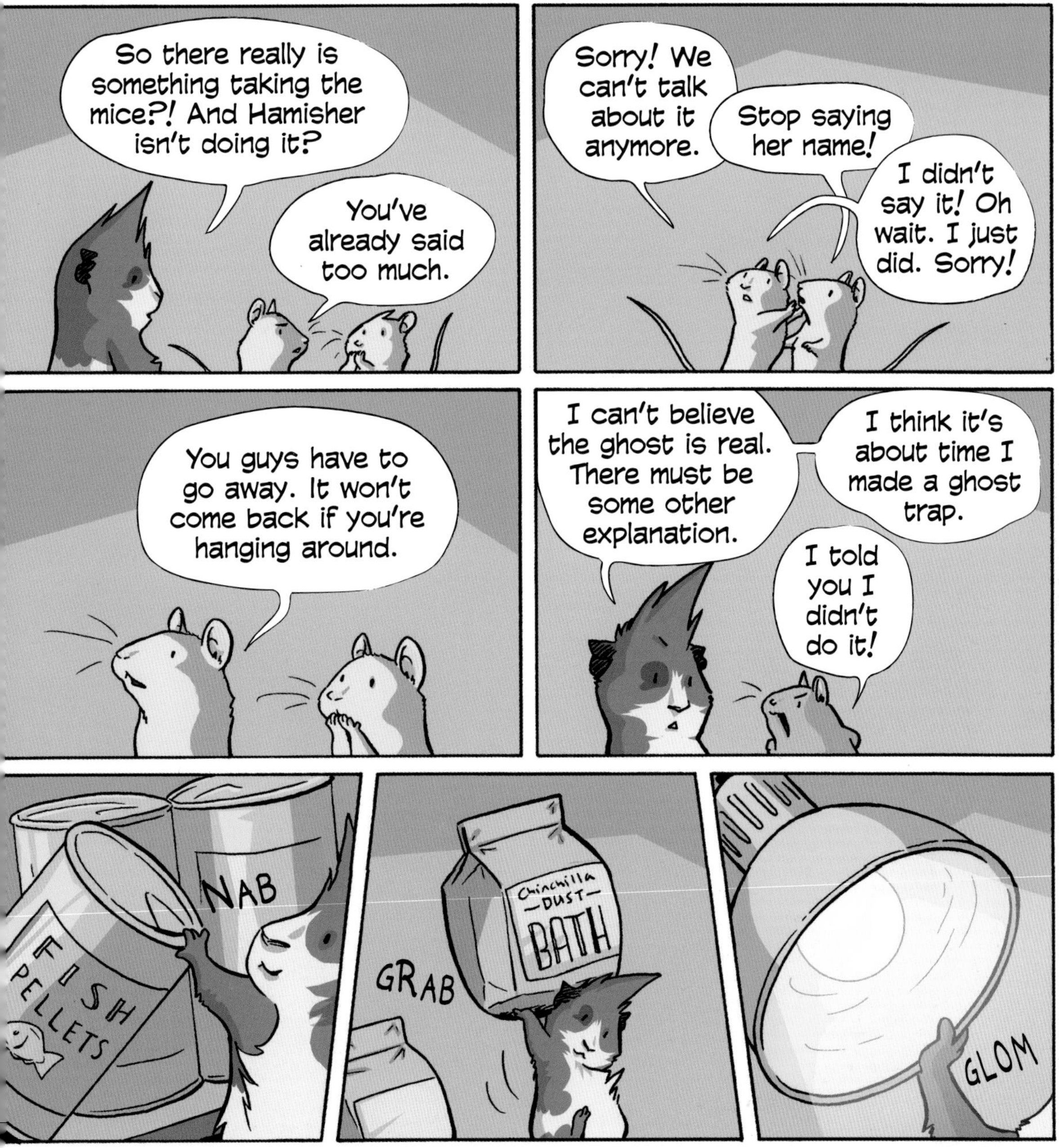
So there really is something taking the mice?! And Hamisher isn't doing it?
You've already said too much.
Sorry! We can't talk about it anymore.
Stop saying her name!
I didn't say it! Oh wait. I just did. Sorry!
You guys have to go away. It won't come back if you're hanging around.
I can't believe the ghost is real. There must be some other explanation.
I think it's about time I made a ghost trap.
I told you I didn't do it!
NAB
FISH PELLETS
GRAB
Chinchilla DUST BATH
GLOM

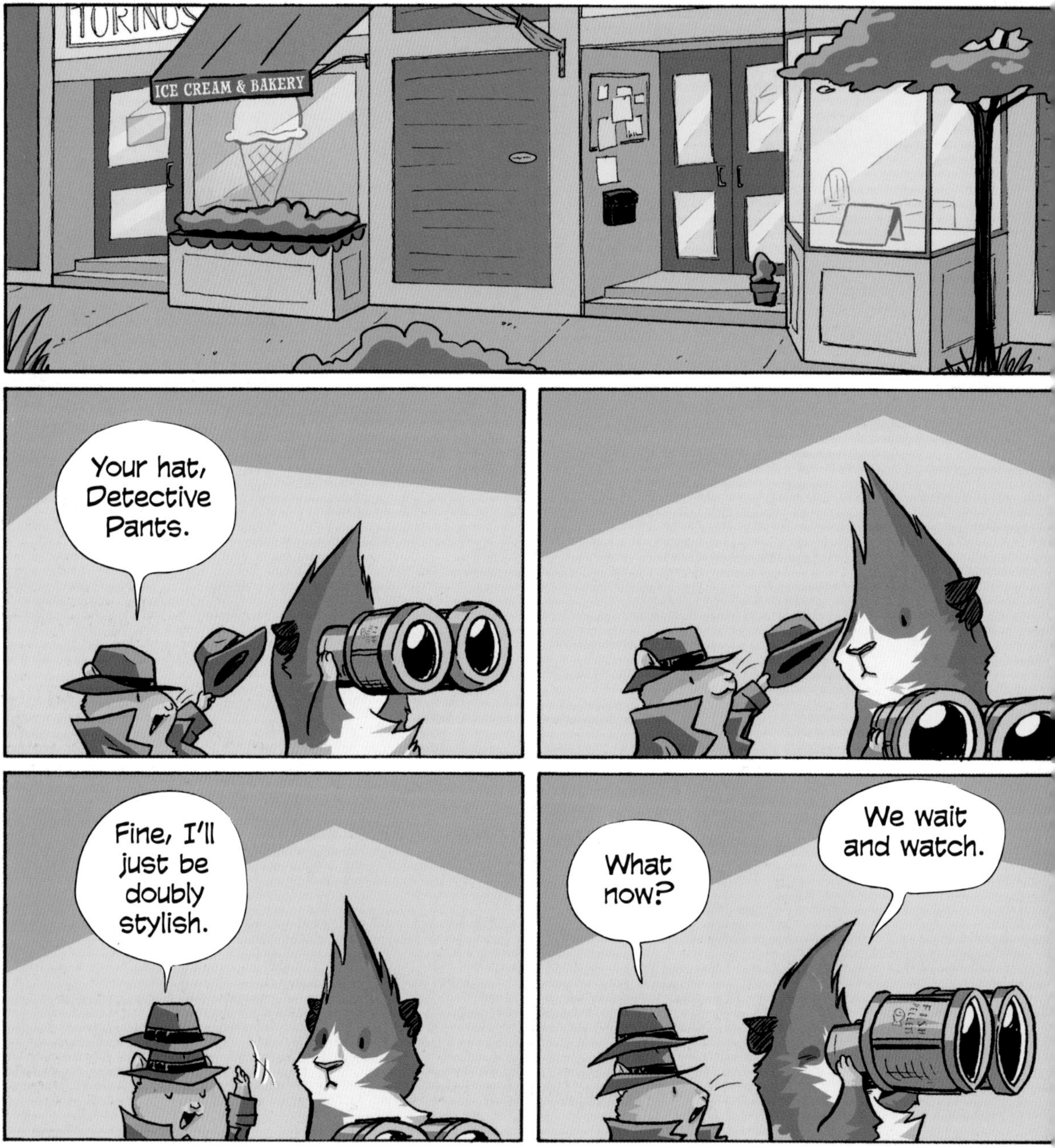
TORINO'S
ICE CREAM & BAKERY
Your hat, Detective Pants.
Fine, I'll just be doubly stylish.
What now?
We wait and watch.
FISH PELLETS

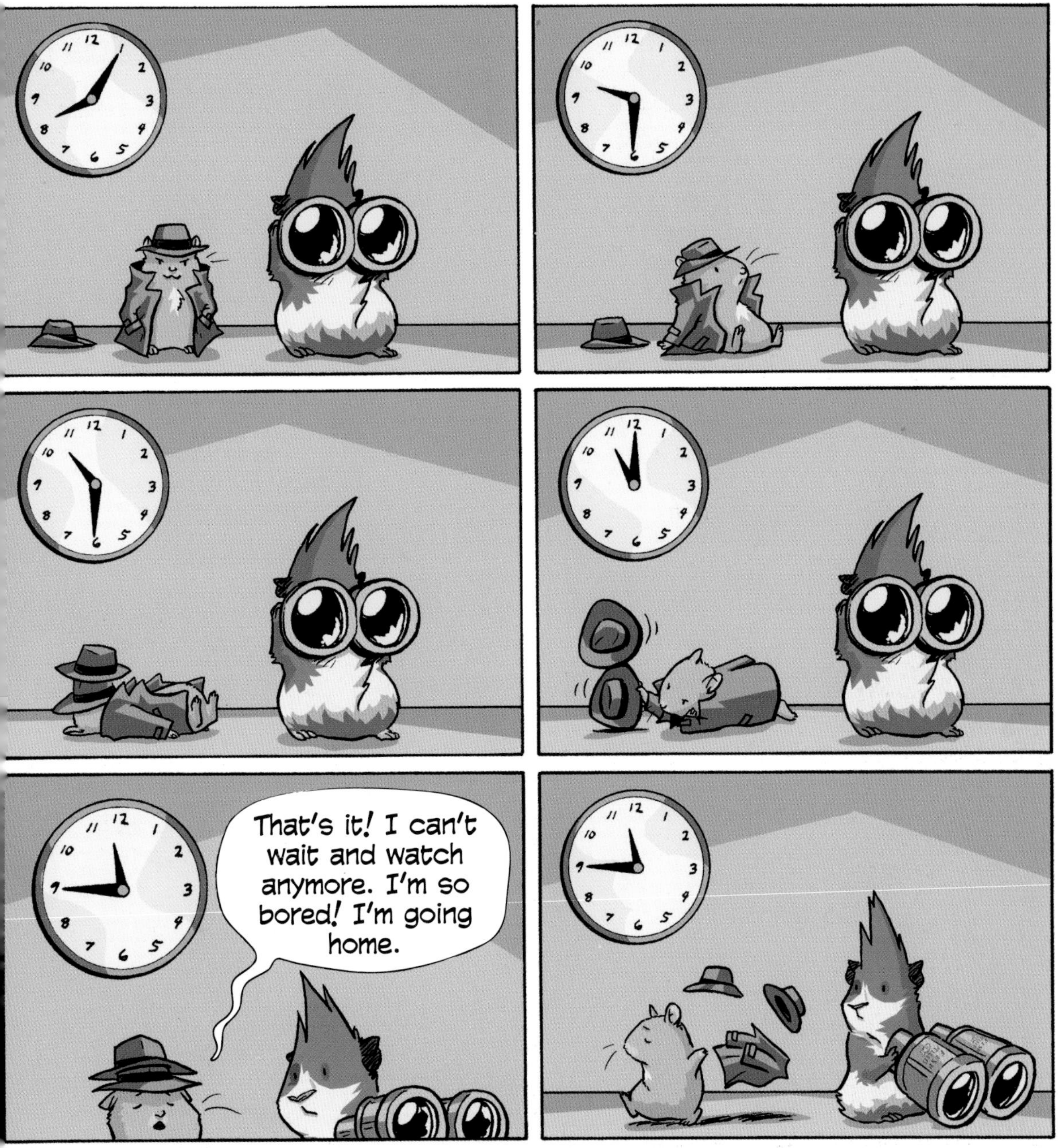
That's it! I can't wait and watch anymore. I'm so bored! I'm going home.

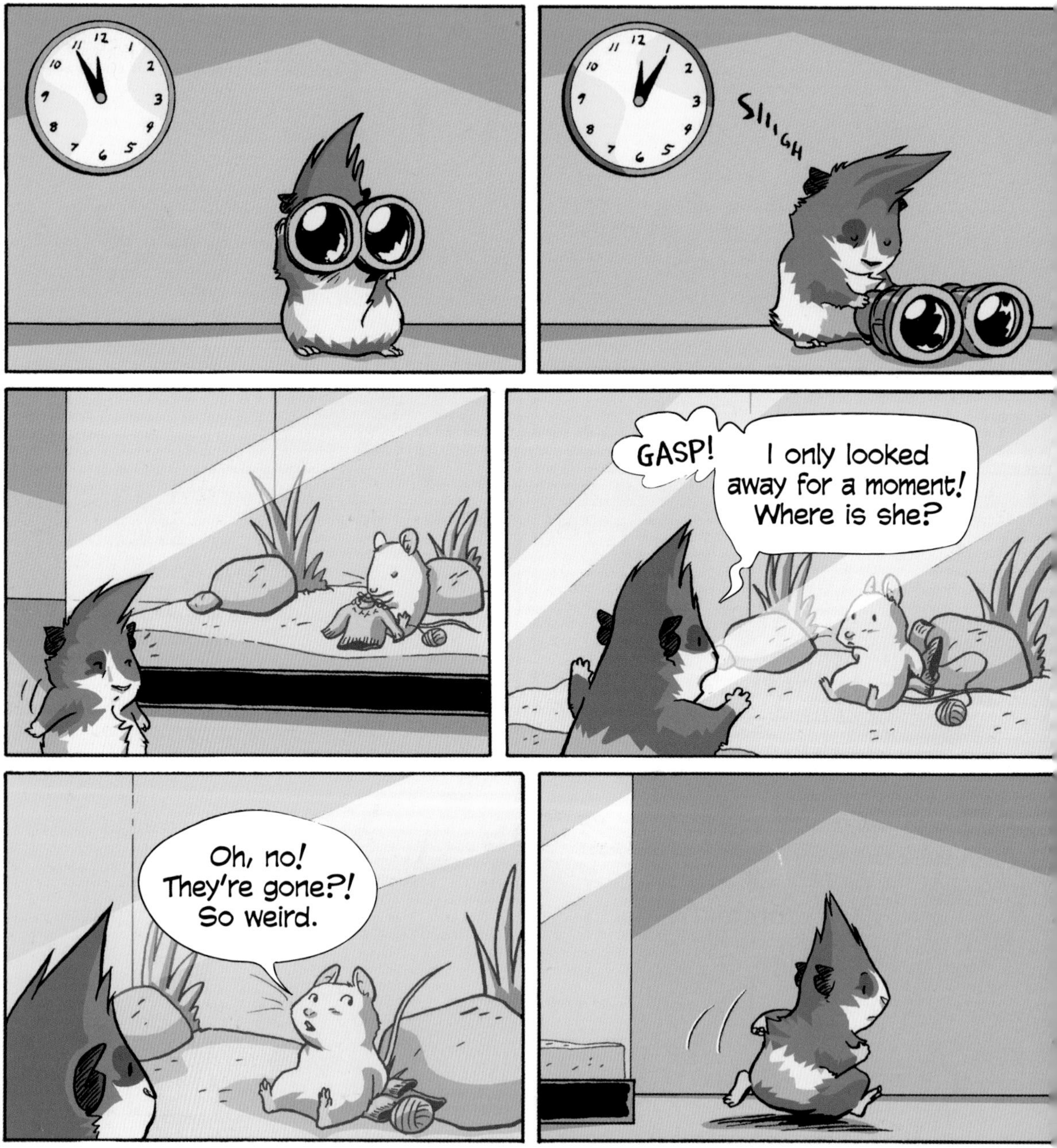
SIIIGH
GASP!
I only looked away for a moment! Where is she?
Oh, no! They're gone?! So weird.

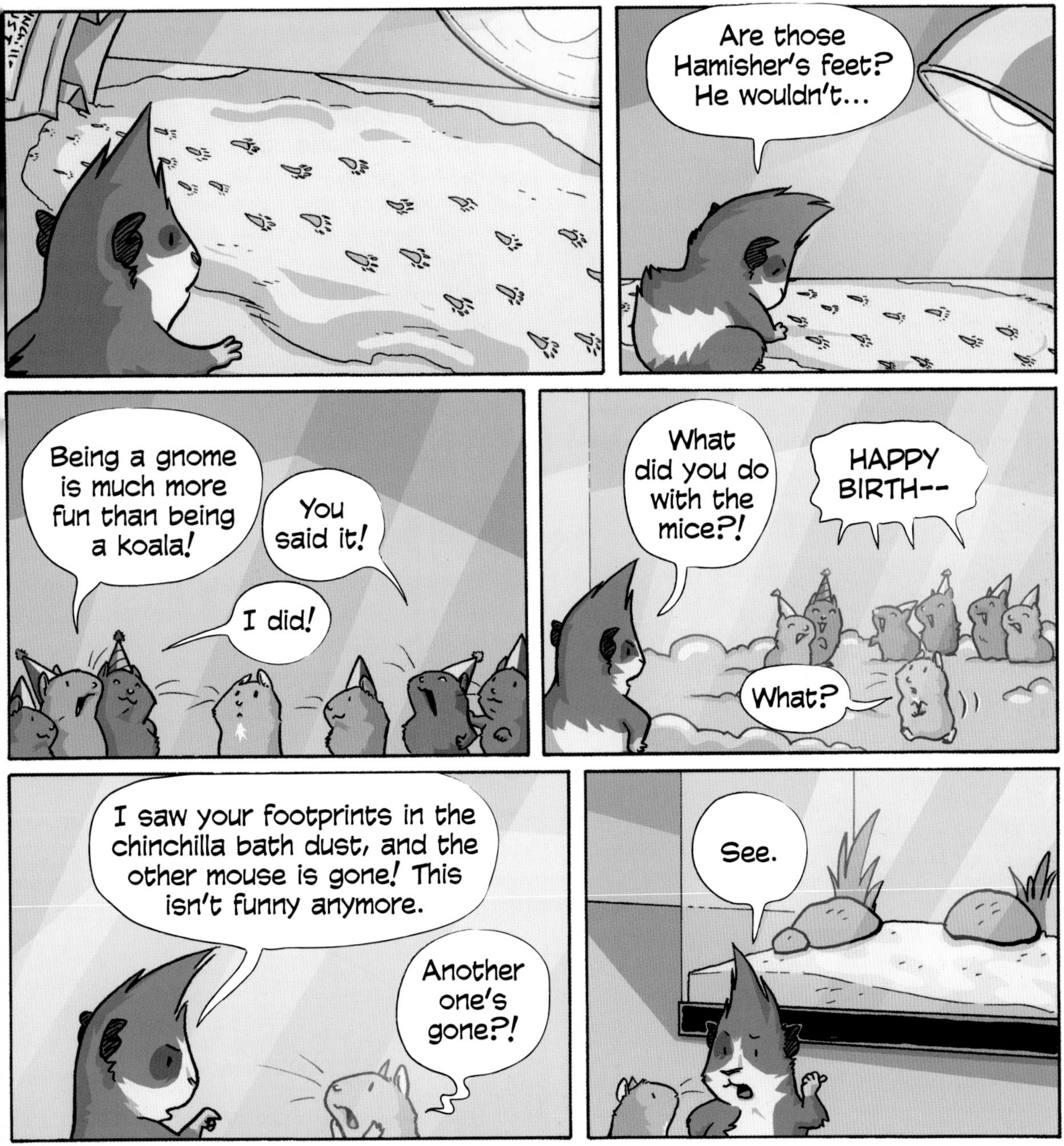
Are those Hamisher's feet? He wouldn't...
Being a gnome is much more fun than being a koala!
You said it!
I did!
What did you do with the mice?!
HAPPY BIRTH--
What?
I saw your footprints in the chinchilla bath dust, and the other mouse is gone! This isn't funny anymore.
Another one's gone?!
See.

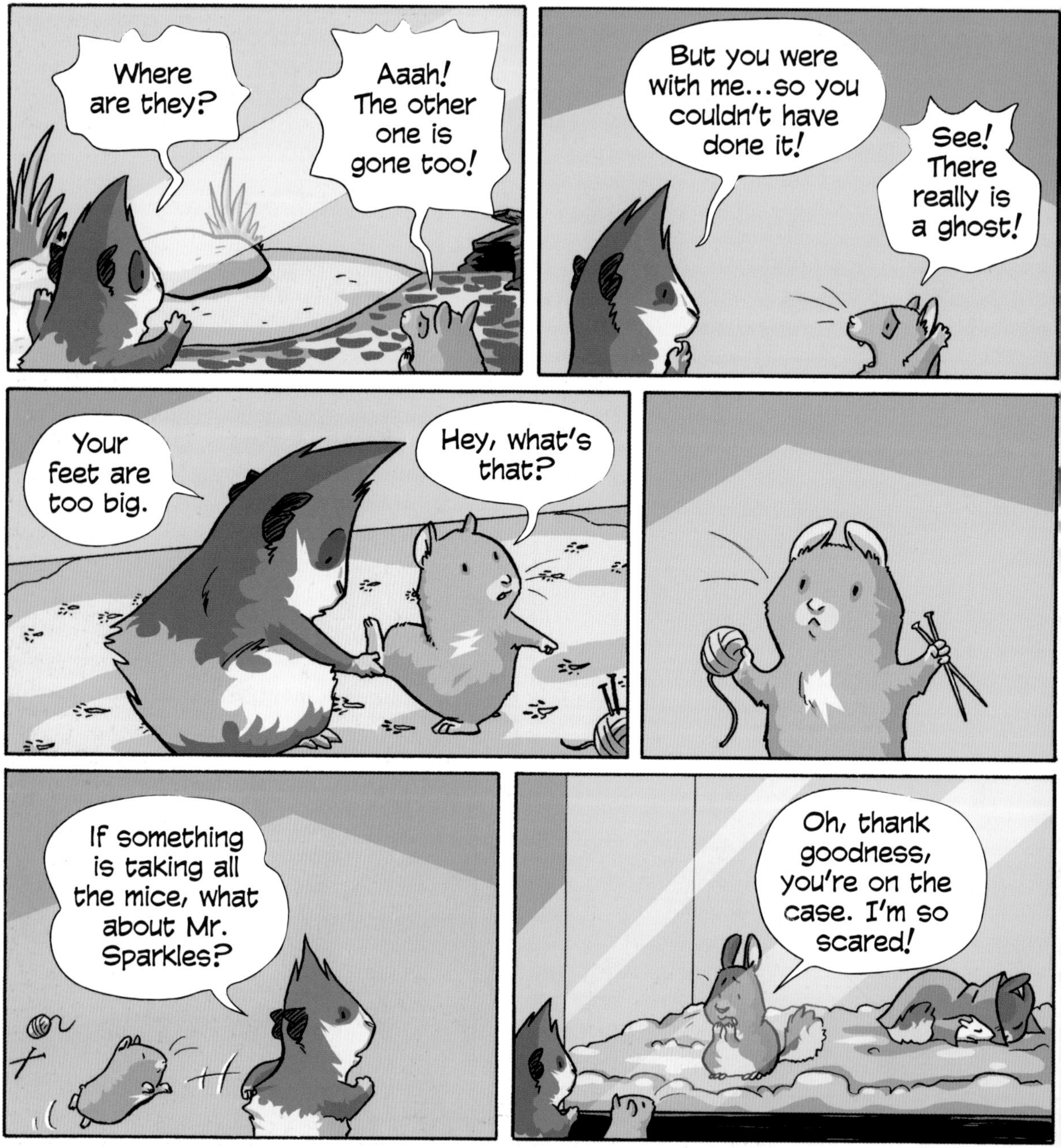
Where are they?
Aaah! The other one is gone too!
But you were with me...so you couldn't have done it!
See! There really is a ghost!
Your feet are too big.
Hey, what's that?
If something is taking all the mice, what about Mr. Sparkles?
Oh, thank goodness, you're on the case. I'm so scared!

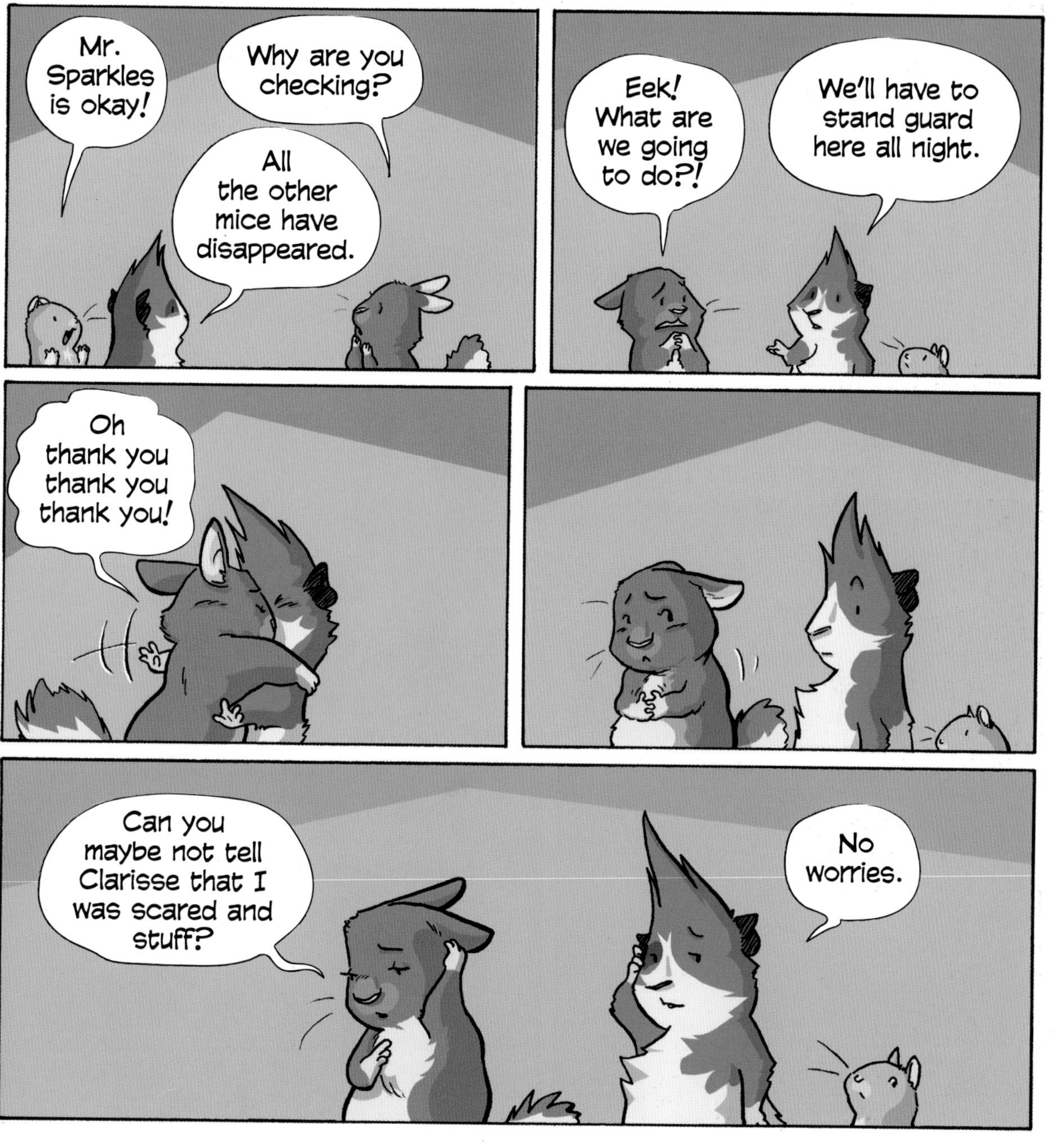
Mr. Sparkles is okay!
Why are you checking?
All the other mice have disappeared.
Eek! What are we going to do?!
We'll have to stand guard here all night.
Oh thank you thank you thank you!
Can you maybe not tell Clarisse that I was scared and stuff?
No worries.

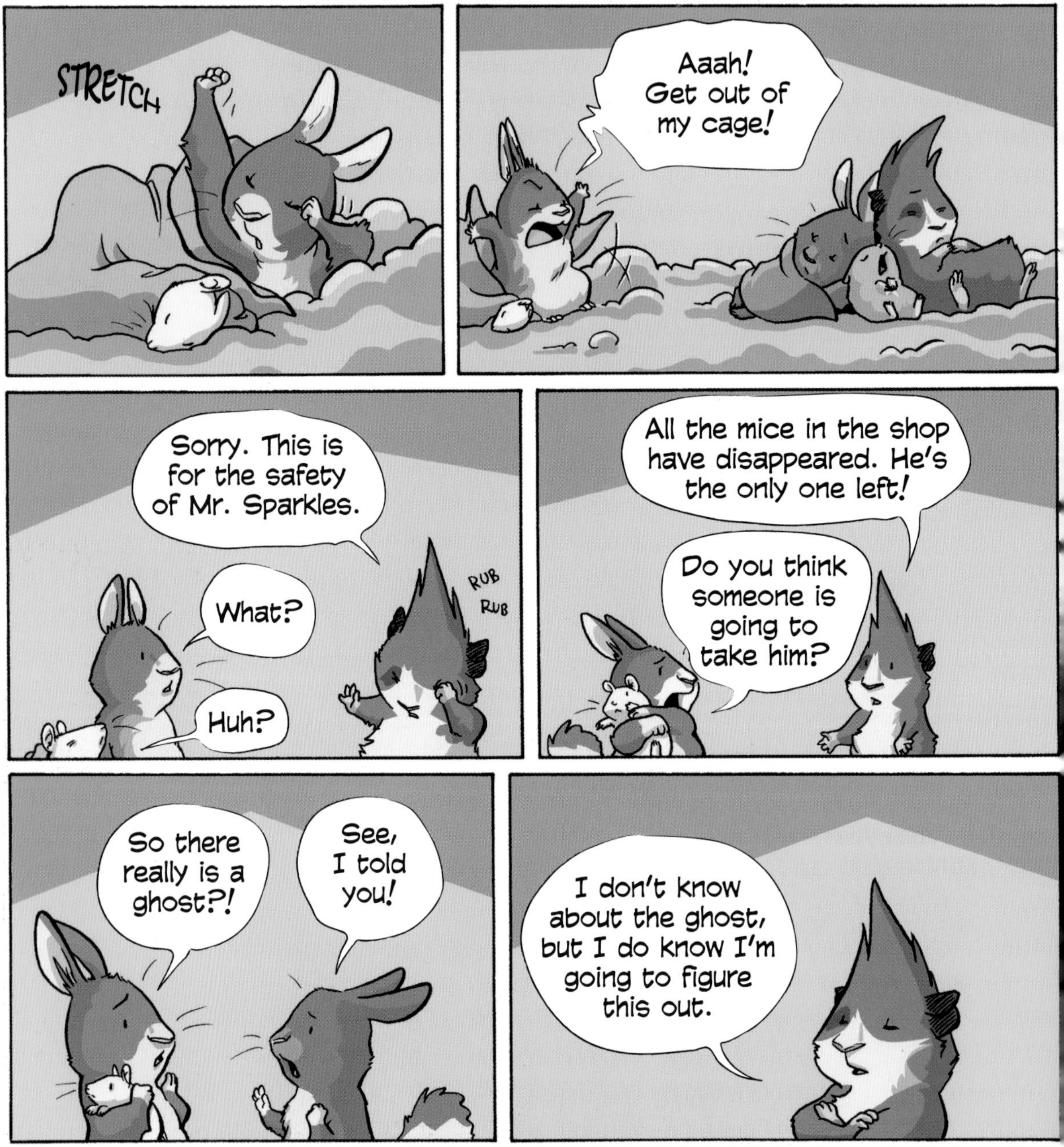
STRETCH
Aaah! Get out of my cage!
Sorry. This is for the safety of Mr. Sparkles.
What?
Huh?
RUB RUB
All the mice in the shop have disappeared. He's the only one left!
Do you think someone is going to take him?
So there really is a ghost?!
See, I told you!
I don't know about the ghost, but I do know I'm going to figure this out.

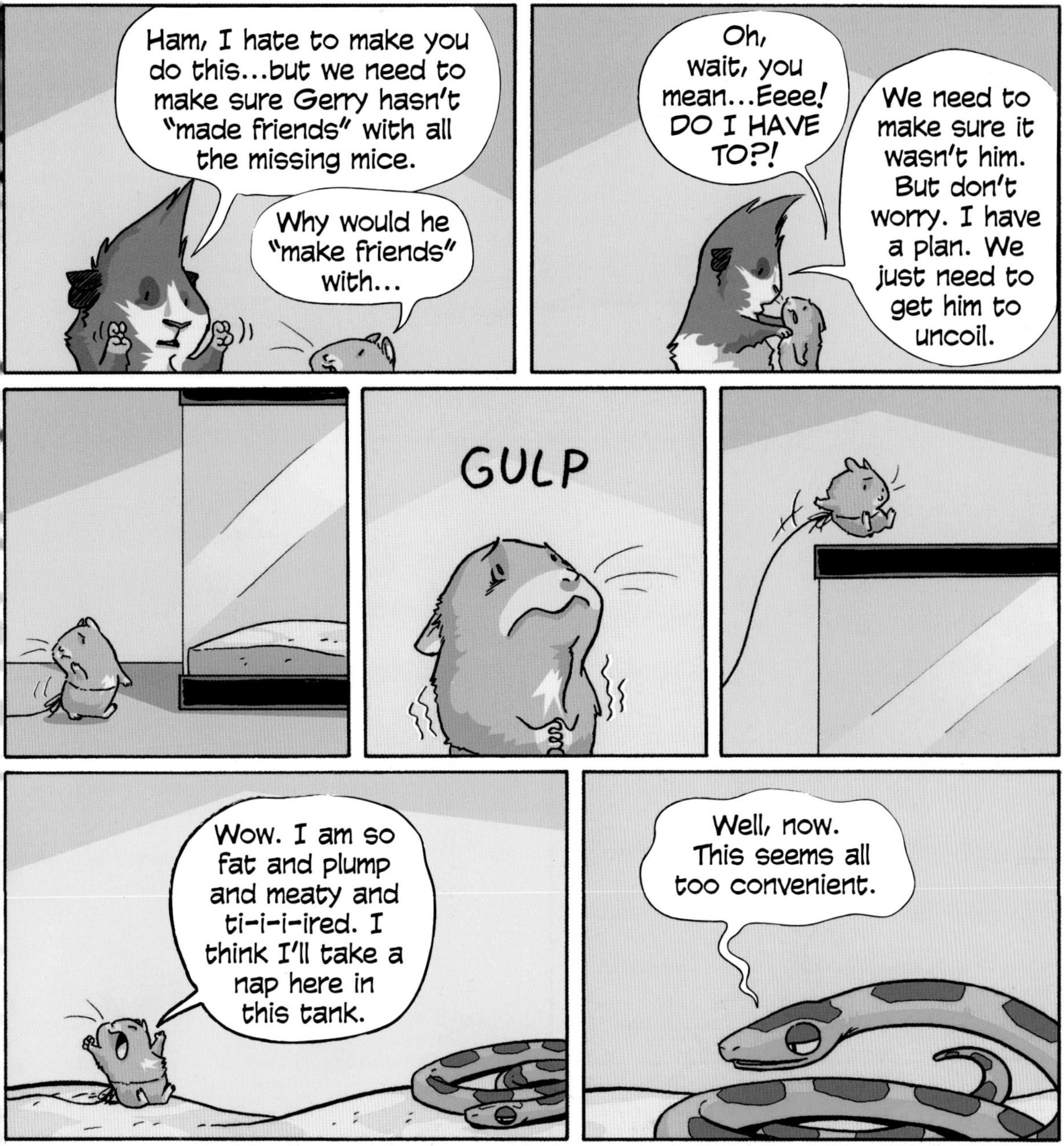
Ham, I hate to make you do this...but we need to make sure Gerry hasn't "made friends" with all the missing mice.
Why would he "make friends" with...
Oh, wait, you mean...Eeee! DO I HAVE TO?!
We need to make sure it wasn't him. But don't worry. I have a plan. We just need to get him to uncoil.
GULP
Wow. I am so fat and plump and meaty and ti-i-i-ired. I think I'll take a nap here in this tank.
Well, now. This seems all too convenient.

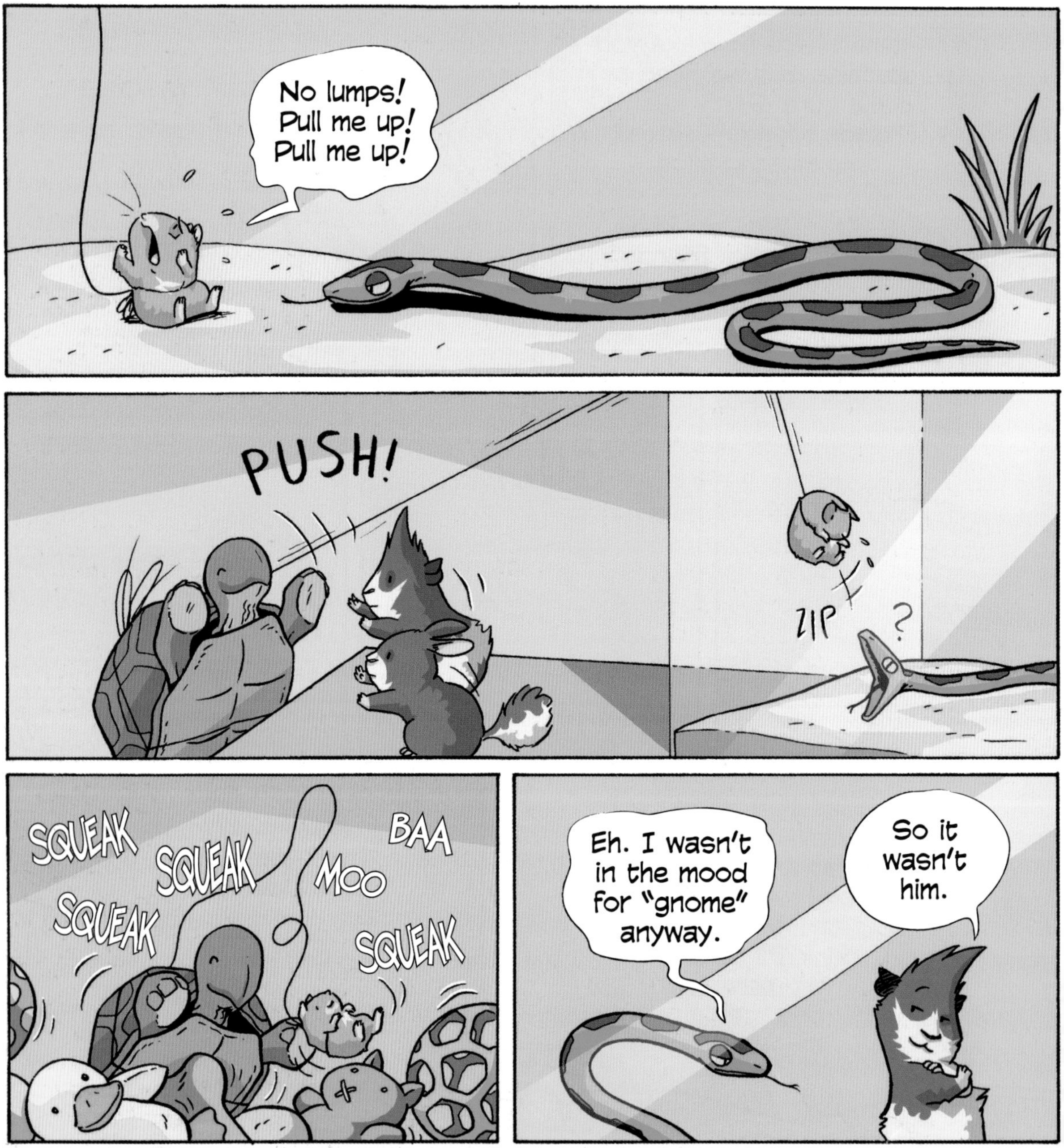
No lumps! Pull me up! Pull me up!
PUSH!
ZIP
?
SQUEAK
SQUEAK
SQUEAK
MOO
BAA
SQUEAK
Eh. I wasn't in the mood for "gnome" anyway.
So it wasn't him.

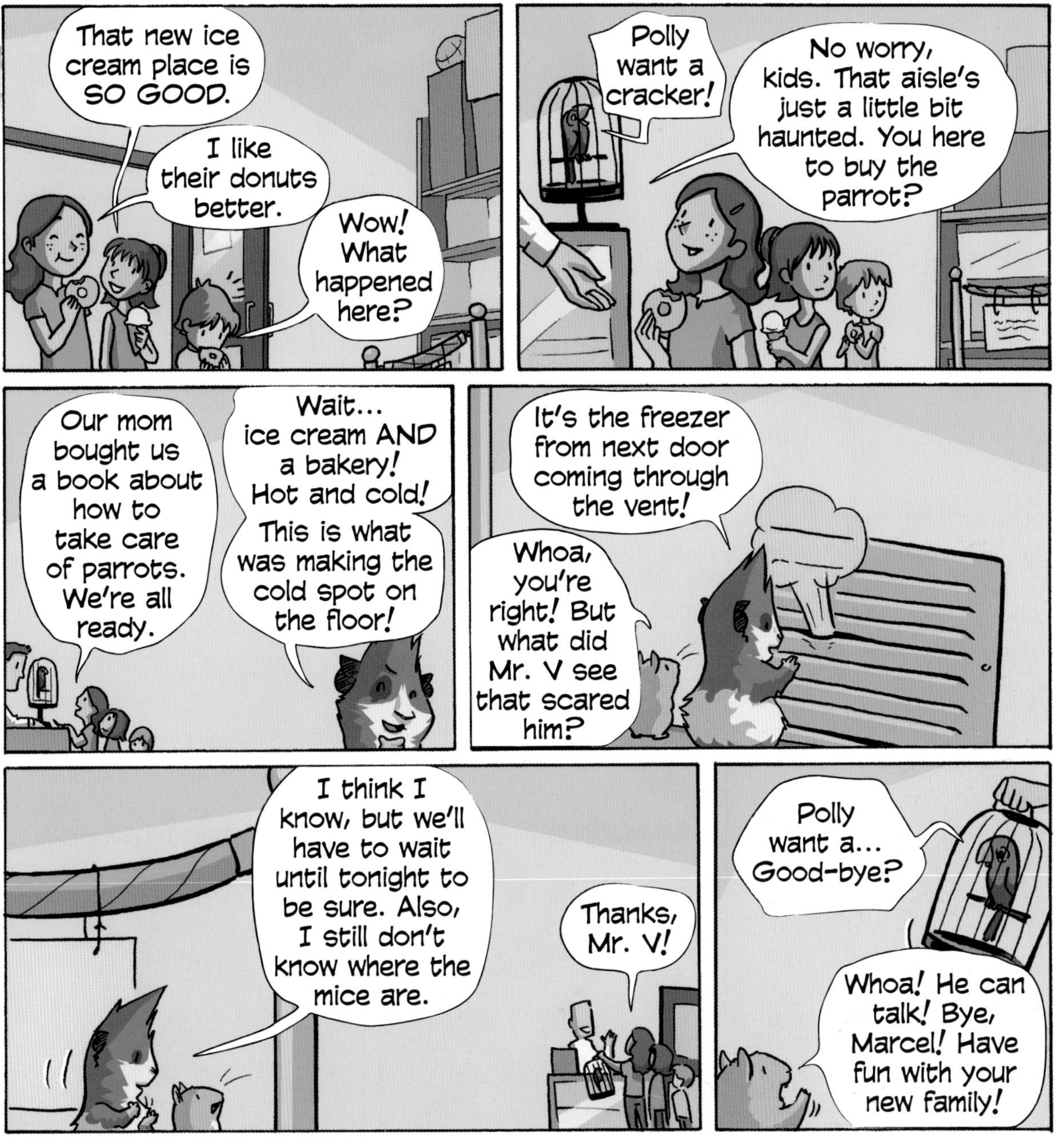
That new ice cream place is SO GOOD.
I like their donuts better.
Wow! What happened here?
Polly want a cracker!
No worry, kids. That aisle's just a little bit haunted. You here to buy the parrot?
Our mom bought us a book about how to take care of parrots. We're all ready.
Wait... ice cream AND a bakery! Hot and cold!
This is what was making the cold spot on the floor!
It's the freezer from next door coming through the vent!
Whoa, you're right! But what did Mr. V see that scared him?
I think I know, but we'll have to wait until tonight to be sure. Also, I still don't know where the mice are.
Thanks, Mr. V!
Polly want a... Good-bye?
Whoa! He can talk! Bye, Marcel! Have fun with your new family!

Good night, my little gnomes.

CLICK

I know you say it's not haunted, but it still gives me the creeps!

My mistake before was that I was using a spotlight. See that light on the wall?

Yeah.

That light is from the heat lamp Mr. V put in the mouse tank. The day he put it there also happens to be the day he saw the "ghost." Keep watching it.

Nothing's happening.

Be patient.

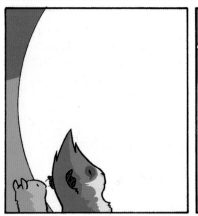

Aaaaahhh!

Just what I thought! The "ghost" is the shadow of the scuba guy from the fish tank!

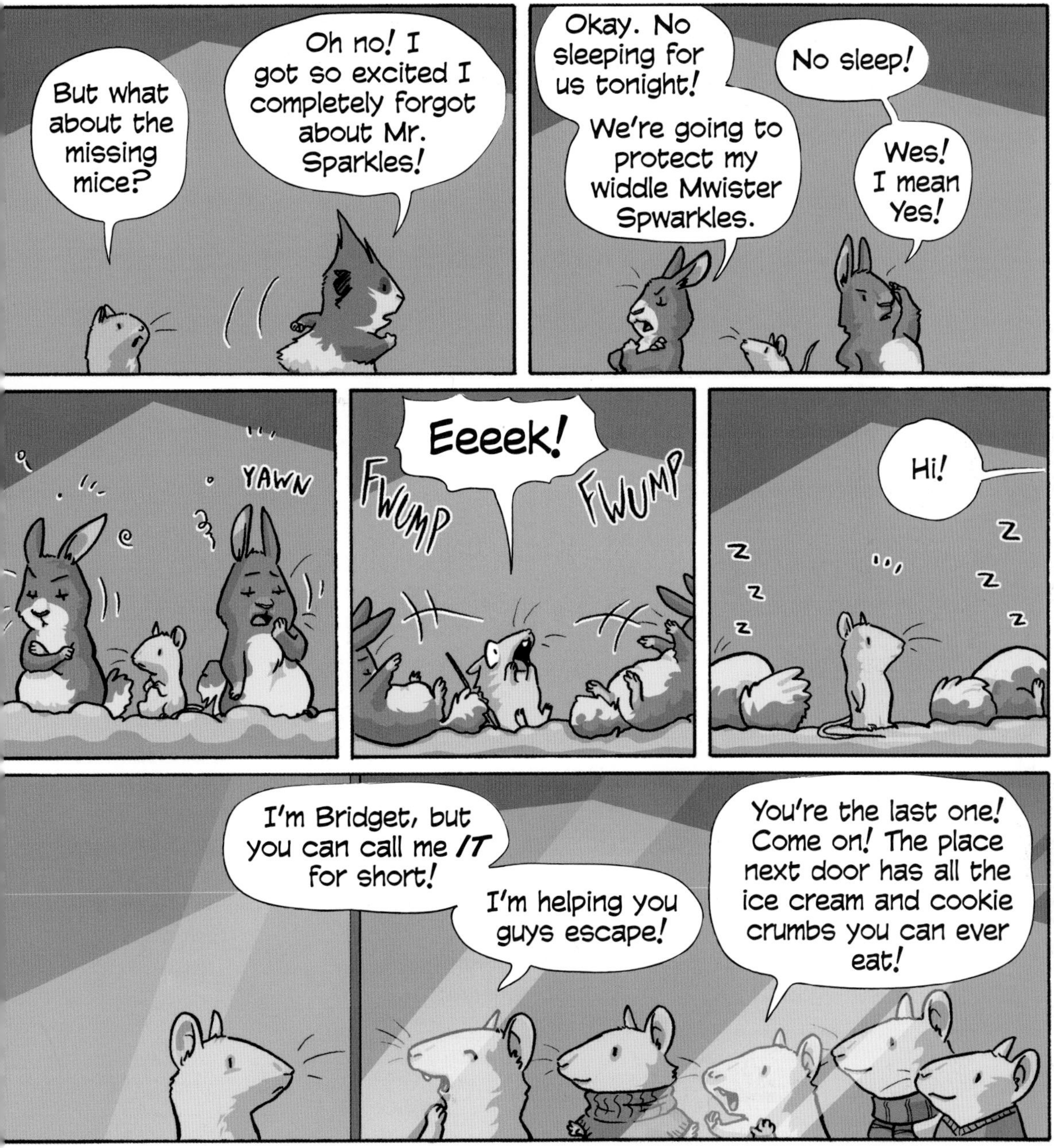
But what about the missing mice?
Oh no! I got so excited I completely forgot about Mr. Sparkles!
Okay. No sleeping for us tonight!
We're going to protect my widdle Mwister Spwarkles.
No sleep!
Wes! I mean Yes!
YAWN
Eeeek!
FWUMP
FWUMP
Z
Z
Z
Z
Z
Z
Hi!
I'm Bridget, but you can call me *IT* for short!
I'm helping you guys escape!
You're the last one! Come on! The place next door has all the ice cream and cookie crumbs you can ever eat!

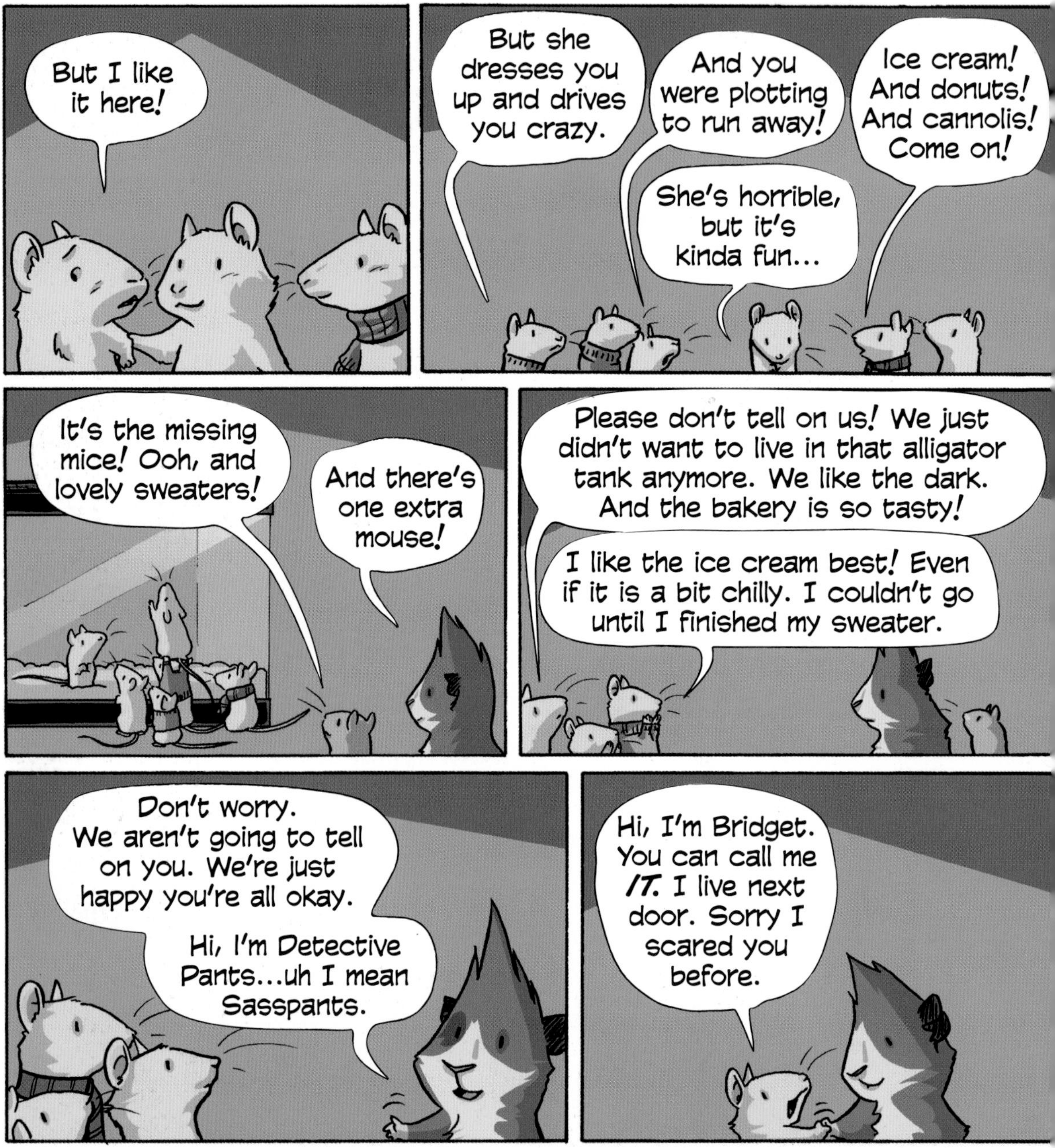
But I like it here!
But she dresses you up and drives you crazy.
And you were plotting to run away!
She's horrible, but it's kinda fun...
Ice cream! And donuts! And cannolis! Come on!
It's the missing mice! Ooh, and lovely sweaters!
And there's one extra mouse!
Please don't tell on us! We just didn't want to live in that alligator tank anymore. We like the dark. And the bakery is so tasty!
I like the ice cream best! Even if it is a bit chilly. I couldn't go until I finished my sweater.
Don't worry. We aren't going to tell on you. We're just happy you're all okay.
Hi, I'm Detective Pants...uh I mean Sasspants.
Hi, I'm Bridget. You can call me *IT*. I live next door. Sorry I scared you before.

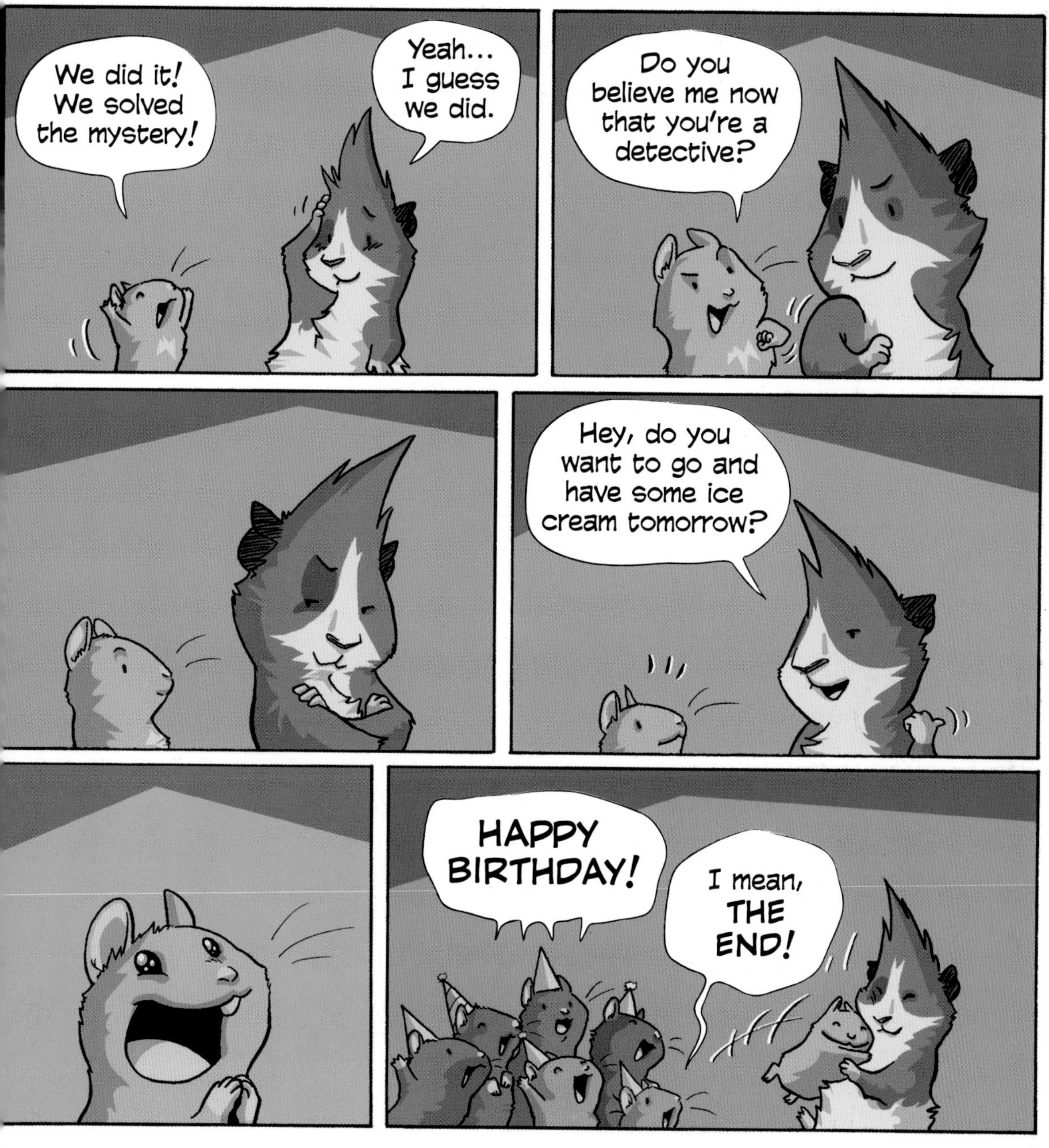
We did it! We solved the mystery!
Yeah... I guess we did.
Do you believe me now that you're a detective?
Hey, do you want to go and have some ice cream tomorrow?
HAPPY BIRTHDAY!
I mean, THE END!

HAMISHER EXPLAINS...

How did the mice get through the walls?

You have to promise me you won't tell them, but some days, I wish I were a mouse. Being a hamster and a gnome and former koala is awesome, and being a detective's assistant is even MORE awesome, but mice have it pretty good! And I'm not just talking about all the donuts and ice cream they're probably eating right now.

For me to fit through that tiny vent, I'd have to do a whole lot more exercise on my wheel. But mice can easily fit through! They can squeeze through a space the size of a dime. They don't even need a vent if there's any sort of crack in the wall!

Also, if I were a mouse, I'd be a lot faster. They run 8 miles per hour. Humans average around 10 miles per hour when they run. Considering a human's leg is two million times the size of a mouse's tiny little leg, that's so crazy! Okay, maybe it's not exactly two million but we didn't have enough mice to pile up next to Mr. Venezi to find out the real number.

Mice can also climb and jump really well! Their tails may look smooth, but they actually have special scales that help with climbing. Mice can run up almost any surface—wood, bricks, really big sandwiches piled on top of sandwiches. Did I mention that mice can even walk upside down?!

Well...it's more like crawling while holding on, but it's still so cool!

Mice live everywhere in the world except Antarctica. I think that's only because they have trouble spelling it.

According to a book Sass lent me, boy mice are called *bucks*, females are called *does*, and—get this—baby mice are called *kittens*. I guess there are only so many words in the world, but that just seems like a baaaad choice! Oh, speaking of words, it says here that the word *mouse* is four thousand years old. I don't even know if Herbert's great-great-great-grandpa was alive then! It comes from a word in an ancient language called Sanskrit, *mush*, meaning "to steal." Mice do make amazing thieves because they can walk through walls...or through cracks in walls.

The book also says that people in ancient Greece worshipped mice. I guess that's before they invented video games. According to legend, the Greeks rewarded mice because a bunch of hungry mice ate the shields of the Greeks' enemies before a big battle. That's why you shouldn't make shields out of cheese!

Oh...wait. It says the shields were leather. Ew. Mice eat leather? Maybe I don't want to be a mouse after all. Actually, I have a feeling they weren't REALLY trying to eat the shields. Mice love to gnaw holes in things, especially when there is food on the other side. Mice can chew through anything softer than their teeth! That's a whole lot of stuff, such as paper and cardboard. If you don't have a dog to blame, you should tell your teacher a mouse ate your homework. Teachers love that!

Mice can also chew through wood, wires, copper, aluminum, tin, and even concrete! That's why you should always make your walls out of something mice wouldn't want to bite. Like smelly socks. Or snakes. Or pictures of snakes wearing smelly socks. I'm pretty sure no mouse would go near that wall!

Animals **NOT** Appearing in This Book and How to Tell the Difference

HAMSTERS VS. GNOMES

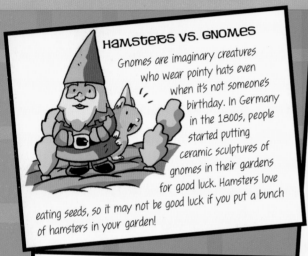

Gnomes are imaginary creatures who wear pointy hats even when it's not someone's birthday. In Germany in the 1800s, people started putting ceramic sculptures of gnomes in their gardens for good luck. Hamsters love eating seeds, so it may not be good luck if you put a bunch of hamsters in your garden!

CHINCHILLAS VS. CHIMNEY SWEEPS

Chimney sweeps clean out dust to make chimneys clean, and chinchillas roll in dust to get clean. The world is upside down! Being a chimney sweep is a very old job. Before houses had radiators and central heating, people had to build fires to stay toasty. Fires make soot, and breathing in soot is bad for you. Chinchilla dust, on the other hand, is great for them! It removes oils from their skin and makes their fur softer. Clarisse may think she's being classy when she dusts, but don't tell her that chinchilla dust is really made from concrete. She's bathing in sidewalk dust!

HERMIT CRABS VS. TRACTORS

A hermit crab may seem like a boring pet, but they are actually very cool. When they get too big for their shells, they move into a bigger shell. If you have a hermit crab as a pet, you can choose the new shell. The word *hermit* means "someone who likes to be alone," but hermit crabs love to live with other hermit crabs. In the wild, they live in groups of 100 or more...though it might be hard to convince your parents to let you have 100 crabs as pets. Tractors, on the other hand, don't seem to care if they have any friends at all!

MICE VS. ALLIGATORS

You can tell the difference between alligators and crocodiles because alligators have U-shaped mouths, but crocodiles have V-shaped mouths. You can tell the difference between mice and alligators because you are smarter than Mr. V! It's one thing to have a house with a mouse problem and a whole other thing have a house with an alligator problem. Eek!